Okay so Your Wife isn't that Good...

Get back in My Bed!!

Alisha Lives or Does She?

The Clean-Up Woman Chronicles

2

Copyright 2013 Holloman

ISBN-10:

0-9897274-0-8

ISBN-13:

978-0-9897274-0-2

Special thanks to

My Aunt, mom, children, and friends that
have supported and encouraged me

This book is dedicated to

All the women that choose to be the other
woman, mates that cheat, and those hurt
by cheating. It's time to doing the right
thing. Journey within yourself and start the
steps towards healing for the man, woman
and the innocent victims(children).

Table of Content

Introduction

When I started writing I was to tell of the pain a young woman suffered but could never overcome because of hurt and shame. Struggling with the fact that she did not want the man she had given herself to after a few months. After a life changing tragedy her thoughts were shifted and her desire changed. Lately desiring someone to grow old with consumed her thoughts. The first book had to be rewritten because her story was not complete as her life begun to transform. Let's continue her journey in this fictional adaption.

Every unavailable man whom I've dated or had sex with taught me something and I was thankful for it. I know women are turning up their nose and saying I shouldn't go after them if they are taken but I never did they came to me and telling them to go home was not my job. I don't believe a woman should chase a man; but a man should respect what he has at home so it's not up to me to enforce his decisions but when I'm done I send them home with a stronger desire to please his mate unless she's not willing to be pleased. Remember I don't deal with men that cheat all the time.

Sex with unavailable men became addictive to me so like any addict I had to go cold turkey, but the more I tried to stay clean the better the men looked and the harder they tried. The high I got from pleasing a man and giving him what he couldn't get at home was unbelievable but when I saw the hurt in another woman's eyes from the betrayal of her husband it was not worth it anymore. It took me falling in love with Malcolm to see being the other woman isn't enough and being betrayed hurts. He never cheated on me but after I fell in love with him I had the ability to understand emotions so that caused me to have empathy for women seen or unseen. Like a junkie I struggled because of the high but the daily reminder to love people kept me clean.

This is not a religious book but the life we live behind closed doors causing us to put our flesh first affects our life as well as others. Everyone's story is different. I decided to live a life pleasing to God and not myself by abstaining from the desires that drive me which included giving up unavailable men. I struggle with that fact so as I walk away from unavailable men my lustful desires increases. I was like a drunk drinking their liver away until the day they would wake up incurable.

You too can have that same remission but you must believe and repent. Now for those with other beliefs seek within yourself for your personal rekindling.

Desire

As I was reflecting and writing in my journal the doorbell rang. "Who is it now?" I said to myself. Walking to the door I checked on Milagro to ensure she was still asleep. When I opened the door my heart leapt as the person standing at the door yelled out, "Surprise!"

"Julian what are you doing here? You scared me." I said holding my chest because my heart was beating so hard from fear.

"Hey Alisha, I need your help."

"Come in and have a seat."

"Oh, here I found this box on your porch."

"What's going on Julian?"

"She left me. She just took the kids and left."

"Why what happened?" I asked in shock.

"I came home after a two day business trip and she was gone but these divorce papers were on the bed, it said final."

"But why Julian were you guys having issues?"

"I didn't think so but about six months after we got married she started hanging out with this group of stuck-up socialites. After two years she quit working and got a full time nanny. She expected me to attend all of these different fundraisers and benefit dinners after she became popular but I hated being there with those stuck-up people. Alisha I just need to know why she left me so I can have closure."

"Julian, are you here for my professional services or as a friend?"

"As a friend but I'll pay you with a round of golf."

"If you pay me with anything I'm not your friend I work for you."

"Let's talk while we play a round of golf."

"Okay I have to take Millie to Alonzo's parents' house for the weekend."

"I forgot you had a child but you named her Millie?" he frowned

"No I named her Milagro Vida but we call her Millie."

"Oh you named her after the singer that sings that back in love song."

"No, Ma Carrie and Alonzo's mother couldn't pronounce her name so they called her Millie."

"Why did you give her a Spanish name?"

"Because I didn't think I would have a child so she is a miracle of life."

"Was Alonzo okay with you giving her a Spanish name and did you at least give her his last name?"

"What do you mean?"

"Well some men want the chil...never mind that's my issue."

"She has our last name Coleman-Avery but come on into the family room and have a seat and relax."

"That's cool but how did Thomas feel about you marrying another man?"

"I'm not married to Alonzo he just adopted Millie."

"Oh so who's the father Thomas?"

"No, oh that's right I never told you how I got pregnant and it's a long story that ends with he was married." I said as we laughed. Julian knew I always ended up with unavailable men and wanted me to set the bar higher.

"I still can't believe Thomas didn't ask you to marry him."

I decided to change the subject because I didn't want to focus on me. "So where should we start?" I asked as I picked up a pad and pen. I asked the first question, "Do you want your wife back or is it over?"

"I don't know. Do you have anything to drink?" He asked looking around.

"No."

"Well, can we go get something to drink?"

"No we are going to sit down, figure this thing out and write a plan."

"Write a plan about what?"

"You and what you desire at this moment in your life."

"I know what I want the same thing I wanted the night I asked Rasheda to marry me." He said smiling.

That was a night I would never forget because we had sex but because he asked her to marry him I was a little hurt. I found out later his mom had given him the ring for Rasheda.

"Julian let's do this. Close your eyes and think of the things that caused you to laugh." I said this to make him focus while changing the subject.

"When I dance more importantly the night I danced with you. Are you and Alonzo together?"

"Julian this is about you not me."

"No this is about me making a mistake because of you and my mother." Rasheda ended up cheating on Julian because she would attend charity dinners alone and caught the eye of another man who had more money but was married. Julian didn't want to face the truth or the possibility that his children may not be his. According to his mom, she told me while we were having our semiannual breakfast date.

"Being with the one you love is not a mistake Julian, we all have choices."

"Yes and that night I chose..."

I became defensive so before he could finish I interrupted. "Julian you gave her the ring that you carried in your wallet for over a year."

"No I didn't I had a different ring but my mom had a ring for me to give her that night." Julian pulled out his wallet and said, "See your favorite color pink and its inscribed."

"Julian you could have just bought this ring. We are friends and that's it but I will be here for you." As Julian sat back on the sofa he gave a hard sigh.

Julian had never acted like this since we stopped having sex I knew Julian was hurt by Rasheda's actions so he needed validation. Before Tommy's first visit Julian and I played golf twice a month and would go dancing from time to time. I was trying to think of a plan of action when the phone rang. "Hello Mrs. Avery. Okay that would be fine." I hung up the phone and Millie begun to stir around in the playpen. It was almost time for her lunch. "Julian I'll be right with you I need to feed Millie and get her ready to go."

"That's cool Alisha I'm going to sit in the

backyard until you finish." He walked out while dialing his phone. I picked up Millie and put her in the high chair when my phone rang again. "Hello beautiful."

"Hi Alonzo how are you?"

"I miss you and my little princess so put her ear to the phone." Millie made unrecognizable sounds because she was talking so fast while she talked to Alonzo. I grabbed the phone in excitement. "Alonzo when are you coming home because we need to talk and I would like to..."

"Wait I'm..."the sounds were muffled but I tell it was a feminine voice in the background.

"Who is that, Alonzo?"

"Baby I'll be home tomorrow but I'm late I gotta go." When he hung up the phone images of him with another woman flashed through my mind. Could Malcolm be right was that picture real was it possible for him to get anot...Millie drew my attention with a scream so I continued feeding her. I focused on Millie and pushed out my feeble thoughts. I finished feeding Millie and took her upstairs to pack her bag. "Daddy's coming home tomorrow and he misses you." She answered with a cheer of "Daddy" as she clapped. My life was perfect with me and Millie but I was ready to settle down.

About an hour later the doorbell rang it was Alonzo's parents. His mom didn't care for me but she adored Millie. Julian's car was gone and I only had fleeting thought to his whereabouts. "Hello Mrs. Avery, how are you?" I said but she ignored me as usual.

"Hey my Millie mouse I've missed you." Mr. Avery came in behind her. "Hello Alisha, how are you?"

"Hello Mr. Avery I pray all is well." I said as he hugged me. Mrs. Avery would only acknowledge me if she had no other choice and because I loved Alonzo I could overlook it.

Elaine Avery didn't like any of the women Alonzo dated and hated his ex-wife with a passion. She loved her grandchildren and Alonzo was her baby boy who could do no wrong. Carmen her only daughter didn't want kids and Cameron her son the oldest child lived over 800 miles away. His wife, Heather, didn't care for Mrs. Avery. Heather and I got along well and the meaner Mrs. Avery was to me the more hell she received from Heather. When Mrs. Avery found out Alonzo's kids were not his she didn't care until she couldn't see them anymore; which devastated her, so she put everything into Millie.

They gathered her things and Mrs. Avery flew by me before I could tell Millie goodbye. Mr. Avery thanked me and apologized as usual for her behavior before he walked out to walk to the car with Millie's bag. He turned and asked, "Are you picking Alonzo up from the airport?"

"Yes but what time does his flight get in?"

"Two o'clock in the afternoon. Take care Alisha and I'll see you guys tomorrow." He said with an apologetic look.

"It's alright Mr. Avery see you tomorrow." I watched as they drove down the street and closed the door.

I decided to go into the living room and retrieve the familiar package I placed out of Julian's sight that I had placed on the table. Why would he be sending me a package now; I thought. I opened the package as I walked into the family room and the only thing contained in the box was a DVD with a sticker that said "PLAY ME". I put the disk in and before I could hit play on the remote the doorbell rang. I got up to answer the door, "Where did you go?"

"I went to the store because your house has prohibition laws that I don't agree with." He laughed.

"Julian I don't drink but I let people drink if they want."

15

"Let me make a drink and we can talk about my future." Julian went in the kitchen to make his drink. He yelled into the living room. "Hey Alisha you want me to make you one?"

"Funny Julian," I said as I thought about the night Malcolm gave me a drink. I would never forget that night suddenly fear overcame me. I quickly pushed aside those thoughts replacing them with my little Miracle of Life. "What are you smiling about?"

"Just thinking about the beautiful results of the last drink I had."

"Alisha, have you gotten sentimental on me?"

"No I haven't but that's when I got pregnant with Milagro."

"The dude got you drunk or did he slip something in your drink?"

"He gave me a drink and I didn't know it had alcohol in it."

"Oh who was tha...wait you mean to tell me your child is a product of rape?"

"My child is a blessing. So let's talk about your future."

Julian leaned back and looked up at the ceiling as if searching for a lost moment within the paint. "I want to date other women and be the man I was before I met her."

"Now Julian you know that will not work you've gotten wiser and you still love her."
"Well I want to experience something different." He said before taking a sip
"How about dating as multiple women but refraining from any sexual contact?"
"Hell no a man needs to release that pent-up frustration." He yelled jumping up
I stood up and caressed his back. "Julian you need to have a meaningful relationship with a woman that causes you to adhere to a certain standard."
"Look I love sex and you know that but spending time with a woman without it is crazy.
"We do it."
"That's different you have always been so much more to me than a woman to have sex with but if you let me I would hit it." I playfully pushed Julian and we laughed.
I was a little jealous when Julian asked Rasheda to marry him but I knew he loved her and I was not ready to get marry.

I picked up a pad and pretended I was taking notes. I was thinking about what Malcolm had said about Alonzo and if Julian really wanted marry me instead of Rasheda. Was I the familiar rebound or am I wishful thinking because of the pictures. I was in deep thought so I didn't see Julian

hook his phone in to the stereo until he grabbed my hand. "Come on Alisha let's dance like old times."
I began to forget my thoughts and started laughing and dancing. We danced all over the living room.

We danced for about twenty minutes when he pulled me close as the music slowed down. We danced for about two more minutes before my body begun to remember and my mind started flashing images of our past adventures in the bedroom. I thought wait Alisha you can't do this you don't cheat remember but Alonzo didn't make a commitment before he left; yes he did he gave me his word about seeking help. Is he seeing another woman and she is carrying his child. "Nooooo" I screamed in my head to hush the thoughts. Before I could pray Julian started kissing me and I responded with my tongue twirling around his as my desire began to flow into full passion I pushed Julian off. "Julian I can't do this I can't do this to Alonzo regardless of his actions I can't betray or hurt him."
"I'm sorry Alisha but she cheated on me and my children may not be mine so I needed a familiar trust." Julian sat down on the sofa as if he had a weight around his

neck and held his face in his hands. I cut off the music and I sat down next to him. As I rubbed his back he said, "I loved her and I want my family back." through his tears as he laid his head in my lap and wept. I just held him in silence until his cries were replaced with snores. I eased off the sofa and covered him up with a blanket.

The next morning Julian was gone but he left a note, "I will call you later." I made a few phone calls as I blended some fruit and veggies so I could have a smoothie for breakfast. I sat down and started looking at my reflection journal when my phone rung. "Hello" I heard whispers, "Alonzo?" Before I could get the thought of him dialing me by mistake out of my head I heard a woman say "I'm telling her everything." suddenly the phone went dead. I dialed his number but it went directly to voice mail so I called again but it rung twice before going to voice mail. I blew it off and went back to my thoughts. At ten I went down stairs to work out for about an hour. This was my Sunday morning routine but I was off today by three hours. I cut on the internet so I could stream church service but I had a few minutes before services started.

As I sat back on the sofa and remembered the DVD so I picked up the remote and turned the TV and DVD player on. "Alisha I want to say you were right about me I had gotten full of myself and needed to reflect. Will you forgive me?" I sat up because Mikael had been in the media a lot lately and it was good but his demeanor was humble and he spoke like himself. "I will be home for good in a few months and I wanted to try us again if that's alright with you." My mouth dropped because this was not the same man who stormed out of my house. He was more mature with the heart of the man I wanted to marry years ago. Lord I need guidance because I want You to bring my husband to me I don't want to pick him. I watched the service and prayed until my alarm went off to pick up Alonzo.

On my way to the airport the images and words from Malcolm two months ago controlled my thoughts and I was scared. Was I getting what I deserved after all these years of being the other woman so I can't complain but why now? I know the hurt and pain I caused or could've caused if a woman had found out about me. Before I knew it I was pulling up and frantically searching for my loved one like the cars before and behind me. I spotted Alonzo and he seemed to be comforting a woman. I slowed the car down so they could finish their interaction. Suddenly she looked up and ran towards an awaiting car and jumped in, Alonzo carried her luggage to the car and put it in the open trunk. After she pulled off and the coast was clear I pulled up and called out, "Alonzo Alonzo" he walked to the car in a fast pace and put his luggage in the trunk. "Hey Alisha let me drive."

"Okay" I said as I exited the car. "So how was your trip?"

"It was okay but I need to talk to you alone so I told mom to keep Millie until tomorrow."

"What's going on?" I asked in a nervous and unsure tone.

"We'll talk about it when we get home. I..." his phone rung cutting him off, "Hello" When he answered he cut his eyes towards me to see if I was looking but I pretended to stare out of the window. "Yes. No. I can't." And for the next five minutes he talked in code before hanging up. "Alisha your graduation is next weekend right?"

"Yes it is Mr. Avery." I smiled and thought he was going to surprise me.

"Baby I'm so proud of you and I've missed you." He said as he grabbed my hand and kissed the palm of it. "I never realized Alisha how much you meant or how special you are to me until I was gone." I didn't know what to say and since I was not going to confront him without proof so I just smiled. "Oh my god" I said aloud when I thought about the envelope addressed to him that had come a couple of days ago.

"Alisha is everything okay?"

"Yes I just thought about something very important." I said frantically thinking

"Oh really, was it the fact you had a man spend the weekend with you?" He said angrily

"What" I said in shock.

He continued as if he was interrogating me. "My mother said she saw a car pulling out of your driveway when they were pulling up and she said he looked like Millie's biological father."

Once he said his mother I became enraged. "First of all that was Julian not some man and does she even know what Malcolm looks like?" He knew that Julian and I were friends and that we played golf from time to time. "You mean your golf buddy?"

"Yes Alonzo." I said folding my arms. "Your mom doesn't like me and that's fine but when you start accusing me because of her false or inaccurate information it's a problem."

"Baby I'm sorry but I hate the fact you're a contractor and work with these men and because you're so beautiful I know they

can't help themselves." He said with
pleading eyes.

"What about the women?" I barked. I knew
he was trying to butter me up and change
the subject.

"That I wanna watch." He said with a laugh.
I shook my head as I smiled at him.

"It's amazing how many men have the same
fantasy." I replied

"Wait I was joking because I would like to
but then I would get upset watching
another person pleasing my wife." He said
waiting for my response.

"Well that's good to hear." I replied as if I
didn't hear him say wife. I've missed you
baby." I squeezed his hand in response to
his statement and asked, "How are the
sessions going?"

"Oh I've been so busy but we'll talk more
when we get..." Before he could finish his
phone rung so he answered it and talked in
code the rest of the way home. I got out of
the car and went upstairs. "Alisha baby," he
cried out as he climbed the stairs. I
pretended as if nothing happened and
calmly said, "Yes Alonzo."

"We need to talk." He said looking anxious.

"Okay" my heart begin to sink but I was
trying to keep an open mind and then I
remembered the package when I picked up
the mail from his house.

"Baby I had a breakthrough and then I had to stop for a few weeks because of my work load." He pulled me closer. "LeLe baby I love you and you will be my wife soon but I've been asked to help our Foreign Branch build a team." My heart beat slowed down and I felt relieved. He took a deep breath before continuing. "Baby I was so good that they offered me an interim VP position heading up that division so I will leave after we have Millie's party."

"Is that the news you couldn't tell me in the car?" I said smiling

"No, I'm not done but it has to wait because I want to surprise you." He said with a big smile.

Alonzo went shopping and picked up a few things so he could prepare dinner. We ate in the backyard picnic style with candles under the moonlight. That night when we went to bed and he prepared to do his familiar search his phone rung. He jumped up grabbed the phone and walked out of the room so I turned over and fell asleep. After I had fallen asleep Alonzo walked in the room. "Hey Alisha what's this?" he bellowed. I turned over and saw the familiar brown envelope in his hand. As he pulled out the contents I said, "You got that a few days ago when I picked up the mail from your house."

"Did you open it?" he asked

"Why would I…it looks like the same one Malcolm gave me when he came by my office a couple of months ago." I said trying to get a glimpse of the contents

"Alisha, when did you start seeing Malcolm again?" he asked

"I didn't he came by to asked me to talk to you so he could see Millie." I said as I stood up.

"You never told me that." He said as he inspected the contents of the envelope.

I quickly replied, "Because it was irrelevant I knew how you felt and you were out of town."

"Alisha have you been allowing my daughter to be around him?" he question as if he never heard my last statement.

"Why would I do that?" The brown envelope drew my attention again. "Alonzo what's in the package?"

"Nothing" he said as he turned to walk out the room but he quickly turned around and yelled, "I can't believe you" he threw the pictures at me. I looked at the pictures they were of me and Malcolm in the park with Millie but that never happen. I ran to the closet and got my package and handed them at Alonzo. "What the hell is this?" Alonzo belted

"The pictures Malcolm gave me of you and the woman you've been seeing. The ultrasound of your unborn child is in there too." I looked him in the eyes and said, "I remember when you told me you couldn't wait to have another one while I was still pregnant with Millie but later you told me you couldn't have kids." I stepped back and folded my arms. "Which one is it?" Alonzo shouted, "I don't have any children on the way and I am not cheating on you." He unfolded my arms. "I want you to be my wife." After he said that his phone rung and he walked out of the room to answer it. I sat on the bed and thought that's it. I walked to the door, "Alonzo we are in the middle of a heated discussion so get off the phone or leave." Alonzo ran back up the stairs dressed and picked up his suitcase and walked out the door.

That weekend I graduated and the only person there was Julian and his mother. Tommy called me that morning and congratulated me but I missed Millie and Alonzo. She spent the week with Alonzo at his parents' house instead of his because he had to leave that weekend. "Thanks for coming Julian but I have to leave and go to Millie's birthday party, she turned a year old Thursday." Julian gave me a hug and a present for Millie. His mom kissed me on the cheek and whispered "Things are going to get better." I rushed off to my car so I wouldn't cry in front of them.

When I arrived at the party Millie ran over to me yelling, "Mommy Mommy" I picked her up and gave her a hug. "Hello Alonzo" I said politely
"It's time to sing happy birthday." He said as he grabbed Millie and walked away and I slowly followed. He sat her in a chair and cut out the lights so everyone begun to sing happy birthday. I was pushed aside as if I didn't belong there. I felt like my heart was going to explode from the pain and thought it couldn't get any worse so I kept my cool and stood in the doorway. It was as if she came from nowhere. She walked up to Alonzo grabbed his hand and kissed him lovingly on the cheek. After she kissed him his head shot up like a deer hearing hunters and searched frantically until our eyes met. I ducted behind the wall so I could make a quick exit. After I ducked out and got into my car and drove off. Tears fell and my heart felt like it would explode. Suddenly the words Ma Carrie spoke to me flooded my thoughts so I cut on the radio and enjoyed my ride home.

A few hours later the doorbell rung and I realized it was Alonzo bringing Millie home. "Hey Alisha" he said with down cast eyes "Thanks for bringing her home." I said cheerfully

"Look I'm sorry about what happen my mom invited her over I didn't know she was...Alisha, can I come in so we can talk?" He said stepping closer.

I smiled saying, "Have a good evening and a safe trip." I closed the door and Millie ran to the window, "Bye-bye daddy." Alonzo slowly walked back to his car and sat there for about twenty minutes before I heard him drive off.

Millie was exhausted so I gave her a bath and she put her to bed early. My phone rang but I left it in the kitchen so I had to run down stairs to answer it. "Hello" I said breathing hard

"Alisha, please don't hang up." He said quickly. "I'm sorry I would never disrespect you or our daughter."

"Alonzo you don't owe me anything you moved on with your life and I shall do the..." He quickly responded before I finished. "Baby no I don't want to move on without you I still love you." He sighed and continued, "Okay I did want to make you jealous but I never moved on. The phone calls and the strange stuff baby it was her and my mom trying to force you to leave me. There was a part of me that wanted to see you get upset so you could see how I felt." He paused and it sounded as if he had taken a deep breath. "When I saw the hurt in your eyes...Alisha I am sorry please forgive me."

With a smile I said, "I forgive you but it's over because you missed my graduation. I got my Doctoral Degree and my family was not there"

He quickly replied "Look in your mail box that was the surprise I had for you when I got home and I was going to give it to you after your graduation."

I hung up the phone because he had the power to change my mind. When I went to the mail box and pulled out a box wrapped up in a piece of paper that read, "Alisha today was not supposed to be like this but seeing those pictures reminded me that I am not Millie's biological father and one day she will want to meet him. I took my anger out on you and I'm sorry. After your graduation I was going to ask you to marry me but I allowed my insecurities to destroy us again. I want you to keep the ring because I will do whatever it takes to get my family back."

My reaction to what I had read was halted by Julian pulling up in my driveway. "Julian, you can't keep popping up at my house anytime you want to."
"I know but you're single and I wanted to ask you something." He said smiling
"Yes Julian what is it?" I said looking through his passenger window.
He took a deep breath before he responded. "Alisha," He got out of the car and walked towards me. "Alisha, would you be willing to date me or give me a chance at something more?"
"Wait what." I said a little shocked.
"Alisha I've always respected, admired, loved, and trusted you." He placed his hands on my cheeks and looked into my eyes. "I wanted you to be my wife then but you pushed me away." He held my hand and asked, "Would you be willing to get to know me again but this time without the sex?"
I looked at Julian and I thought about all the men I assumed were right for me and he was the only one that didn't cause drama. I smiled saying, "Yes Julian I will date you." He picked me up and started kissing me as I whispered in his ear, "Can we have sex just once?"
"I know that's a trick question and even though I want to throw you down and

please you now I'm not." I thought darn I need some but he is right we need to wait. Julian jumped in his car and drove off.

A few minutes later my phone rang, "I didn't want to leave like that but I was losing control and I want to get to know you on an intimate level." He paused. "Alisha we were lovers and then friends but now I want more." His tone had changed and I could hear how serious he was. "Baby I never stopped loving you."
When we hung up I thought we are going to both be redounds. I took my shower dressed for bed and dreamed of my new future.

I was awaken by my phone ringing "Hello"
"Alisha, I couldn't sleep baby I can't leave knowing you don't want me. Did you get the package out of your mail box?" he asked nervously.
"Yes" I replied, "It's over I'm moving on and I will send the ring back." I hung up but he kept calling back so I answered the fourth time and heard him out. Alonzo realized the stupidity of his actions because he listened to his mom as usual instead of his dad. Ginger, the woman that kissed Alonzo was the daughter of his mother's best friend Mildred. Ginger and Alonzo dated in high

school but he met Jacqueline his first wife and dumped Ginger. Now after all these years his mother could get them together. She lied to Ginger about Alonzo's feelings towards her. His mother had sent her to the apartment he was staying at to surprise him. She was the female I heard in the background and saw at the airport but the code talk was with his mom calling him about Ginger and because he was a mama's boy he couldn't stand up to her.

I responded with "Alonzo you allow your mom to disrespect me and I don't say a word. This time you allowed her to break my heart now I can forgive you but the forgetting is a struggle, so don't call me anymore. If it's about Millie text and she is never spending the night at your mom's if she wants to see her she can call and set up a day and time. Thank your mom because she finally broke us up and you can be with Ginger Good-bye" I hung up and sent his number to automatic voice mail.

Boyfriend

Before Julian and I decided to date he had already sold his company and became that fun-loving rich kid again but instead of dancing he took up daredevil stunts and decided to get his pilot license; this was revealed on our first official day of dating. I told him before we could get serious he would have to stop all the daredevil stuff. He agreed so we discuss several different issues and came to a resolution for us to move forward in the relationship.

He spoiled Millie and me. Julian wanted me to get a nanny so I could have more freedom at work but mostly play with him. That morning I awake to Julian's call. "Baby get Millie dressed we are going to breakfast."
"Okay but I have clients to see today starting at ten."
"I will take you to work and pick you up." I got up and we got dressed within thirty minutes. Millie was asking for Alonzo so I

began to feel guilty about having another man around until the images of Alonzo and Ginger popped in my head again. I had forgotten Millie knew Julian already but this was different. He rang the doorbell at eight o'clock so I grabbed Millie and we headed out the door. He had bought her a car seat for his car already so I didn't have to take the one I had out of my car. I knew in my heart this was going to be a great relationship. "Good morning baby" he said with a kiss and I reciprocated. He turned his attention to Millie "Hello princess." Millie waved her little hand and hugged him.

As we drove Julian let me know about the nanny. "Baby I will be looking for nanny's today so they will start the one on one interview with you tomorrow. Is that okay?"
"Yes Julian we can do it at my office between appointments." I knew he was a man that did what he said without hesitation and wanted things done quickly because he lived for the moment.
"Sounds great, what time will you start?" he asked
"When we get to my office I can give you a copy of my schedule." I said thinking about my actions and the pace things were

happening. Suddenly Julian blurted out, "I'm going to my favorite place to eat breakfast; is that alright with you?" he said looking straight ahead.

"If it's the Country Break House yes and I'm getting excited just thinking about it." I said rubbing my hands together and licking my lips.

"Good I thought you were on a health food kick like most women." He reached over and grabbed my hand. "I'll never stop loving you" I wanted to say the same thing but my phone rang. "Hey Tommy" I shouted

"Hey Lisha." I could hear him smiling. "How are you and Millie?"

"We are great." I cheered. "We are on our way to breakfast with Julian."

"Tell my golf buddy hello." He changed his tone. "I called to let you know I won't call you for a few weeks because I am going off the grid but you can leave me messages and I'll call you as soon as possible." He sighed as if there was something he wanted to say but couldn't. "I just wanted to say hi and kiss Millie for me. Love you Alisha."

"Love you too Tommy." We hung up and I gave Julian the message. "Tommy said hello"

He quickly asked, "Does he know we started dating?"

"No because that was the first time I've

talked to him since my graduation." Tommy and I talked every day until the past three weeks.

"Are you okay with us being together?" he asked nervously.

"Yes Julian I love being with you." After I said that I remembered he was a quickie. My phone went off as we pulled into the parking space. "You're mighty popular this morning." He said.

It was a text from Alonzo. "It's a text." I said with a grin.

"Well you take care of that while I get Millie and you can meet us inside." He said getting out of the car.

I looked down at my phone and read the text. "Baby I'm sorry you and Millie are my life and I can't lose you I love you. Alisha, please don't leave me like this."

I text, "Lonzo you did this not me. I waited on you and I prayed for us but you allowed a lie to destroy us so now I need time to think and heal."

He text "I just found out I would be gone for six months to a year but I will video conference Millie every day I'm free or at least once a week depending on my schedule." I grimaced because I knew it was hard for the two of them.

"Just text me before you call and I'll email a copy of my schedule today."

"Okay, tell her I love her and will miss her and mommy too." My chest felt funny and I was confused but I brushed it off. When I walked in all I could hear was Millie, "Mommy Mommy" as she ran over to me. I walked over to the table and Julian stood up and smiled. "She is her mother's daughter when she sets her mind on something that's it plus she's feisty."
"She wanted pancakes." I said in a matter fact tone and laughed
"And her Mommy so she jumped out of the chair before I could help her.
"Sorry about that." I said as I smiled
"That is fine I know how she feels I want her Mommy too." Julian smiled "I ordered your favorite"
"French Toast, bacon, scrambled eggs with cheese, and apple orange juice mix?"
"Yes and the princess got mixed juice and pancakes. She speaks well for her age."
"That's because its food." I laughed
"She is definitely like her mommy."

The waiter came with the food. As we ate we talked about our future. After Millie finished she climbed into my lap so we left and went to the clinic. "Julian will you open up and take the baby inside for me because I need to check on Mrs. Steinberg." Mrs. Steinberg would open her blinds and let in some sunshine or sit on her porch to drink coffee as she read the paper every morning. This morning her house was shut tight. I walked over and rang the doorbell but no one answered so I walked back to the clinic to get my key. "Julian will you watch Millie for me?"

"Yes but is Mrs. Steinberg okay?" he asked "I don't know but I'm going in to check on her." I walked over and knocked on the door again before I opened it. When I walked in and found Mrs. Steinberg on the floor I ran over to her pulled out my phone and called 911. "Mrs. Steinberg, are you alright?" She didn't answer but I could feel a slight pulse as I was checking her I was talking to the 911 operator. The ambulance got there within minutes and the police pulled up behind them because of the address. Everyone in the neighborhood loved her; if it was not for her I would not have been able to get the zoning I needed to run the clinic. Julian assisted my client until I could get back. I called her sister and son to let them know where they were taking her after everything was over and locked her house back up.

When I got back to the clinic an all too familiar face was there. "Hello Mrs. Maldad, how may I help you?" I said looking around

"Hello Alisha I just wanted to check up on my step-daughter." She snarled

"Thank you for coming but you can leave now." I retorted

"You said we could have lunch and talk your treat." She sarcastically replied

"Well as you can see I don't have time today." I smiled

"I have paid to see you today and I expect you to honor that." She said hastily

"You also lied about being one of my new patients." Julian pulled me to the side.

"Baby I didn't tell her anything but I'm not leaving until she does. It was just something about her trying to see Millie that I didn't like." He whispered

"Did she walk around in the house?" I asked

"The waiting room is the only place." He said looking at her

"I'll talk to you later about it." I said rubbing his arm to ease his concern

"Be careful she seems strange." I kissed Julian because he was already protecting Millie and me without a second thought.

"Mrs. Maldad, how may I help you?" I asked

"Have you seen my husband?" she snarled again

"I have moved on." I said with smile

"NO! I don't mean like that." She blurted

"What are you talking about?" I asked

puzzled

"He misses you and the baby please let him come by." She quietly asked

"Mrs. Maldad I don't have time for this what do you want?" I asked impatiently.

"My husband is in love with a woman who doesn't want him and its killing him but the worst part is he can't see his daughter." She said with a fake sympathy

"You mean the daughter he wanted to kill well actually both of you tried to kill?" I barked

"That's not fair." She said softly

"Really well that's life. Thank you for coming and have a nice day." I said pointing towards the door.

"You self-righteous bitch how are..."

Julian ran in, "is everything okay?"

"Yes she was just leaving." I said with a big fake smile.

She smirked and said. "We will get the baby."

After it was all over I went into my office and sat in my chair. I was thinking Alonzo is gone and I don't know what to do but I shook it off as I wiped my face. "Julian, help me check everyplace she was sitting."

"Why?" he said puzzled

"I think she planted something in here. Put these gloves on first." We started searching

40

and I found a vile of cocaine in a chair.

"Babe I have a few friends I can call to take care of the situation." He said

"Julian I'm not going to hurt anyone." I said passionately

"No baby I mean legally and give me that so I can get rid of it." He smiled and hugged me

"Yes I would like that." I said with a sigh of relief.

"Okay." Julian pulled out his phone as he walked out the door.

My second appointment was there twenty minutes early and I was glad. Some of my patients had reached a breakthrough and it gives me inspiration to see others flourish in their new found life. When Meredith Chesterfield first came it was for a couple's session but she continued to see me. The issues with sex hunted her for years and even during our sessions her beliefs clouded her judgment so we had to use the Bible to help her receive revelation. The one on one session's were about technique and according to her husband this was necessary. "Hello Mrs. Chesterfield, how are you today?"

"Pregnant" she smiled

"Congratulations how far along are you?" I said covering my mouth.

"Five weeks." We talked as we walked into the office.

"I believe this will be my last session." She squeaked

"Why is this your last session." I asked. Her last session was over a month ago but she wanted to continue so I had to make sure it was her choice.

"I know I'm ready to step out and walk on my own." She said nervously

"Well that's good to hear." I picked up my pad. "What would you like to go over today?"

"I'm not sure as I sit here I believe I used you as a crutch." I knew that and told her but she had to come to that revelation on her own. She hugged me and we talked some more before she walked out of the clinic almost skipping. I had one client left at four and my two this morning didn't last for twenty minutes. After Millie was born I changed my work load so I would only work four days seeing up to twelve people a week and new clients were seen on Monday or Wednesday.

Julian called around eleven thirty to see if we wanted anything to eat and to give me an update on Mrs. Steinberg. I thought Julian does love me but do I still love him or is this just a rebound situation. I sat

down and wrote some things down and
prayed. When Julian got there with the food
I was in the back playing with Millie. "Baby
I don't like the way you leave that door
unlocked especially after this morning." He
shouted through the clinic until he saw me.
"She or even he could come back and I
don't want to lose my precious girls."
"Okay Julian I will lock it from now on." I
smiled. "How, did you know about Mrs.
Steinberg?"
"I went to the hospital to see her and her
son gave me an update he also sent his love
and thanked you for checking on his mom."
Julian and continued talking as we walked
into the kitchen. "Did you forget I helped
you redo this place and I would talk to her
son because of how he looked at you?" We
laughed
"Julian you were with Rasheda so any man
could've look at me back then." I laughed
"Not while I was in your life, I told you I
wanted you to be my wife then and I want
you to be my wife now." I smiled and was
about to kiss him when Millie said "Pray
now." I was about to pray but Julian
stopped me and blessed the food. I knew
Julian had gone back to church; this was
not the man I met or befriended playing golf
he had grown spiritually as well. "I knew if I
came back into your life I would have to

43

come as a saved man so I went back to church after I started playing golf with Thomas." He kissed me on the cheek. Julian turned around and looked into my eyes when he said this. "You counsel people while you hide your own fears and regrets. Alisha I am going to be the man who loves you unconditionally and put you first so all those past hurts will fade away."

"Mommy cry hold baby" Millie said as she reached up so she could comfort me.

"I have her Millie." Julian kissed my hand as he whispered, "Out of respect for the baby I won't hold you yet but you will be my wife." I smiled and thought about our relationship as being a rebound situation. Millie ran off to play after lunch and I ran behind her.

We played with Millie until she fell asleep. Julian grabbed me and pulled me into his arms while kissing me. Still holding me in his embrace he said, "I am spending the rest of the day with my girls." My phone went off it was Alonzo sending me a text about his mom wanting to see Millie this weekend. I let him know I would check my schedule after telling Julian who it was and the situation.

My last appointment was a family torn apart by a possible divorce because the mother was unfaithful and she was having another child by her lover. This was their third visit and the 10 year old son was the only person not willing to forgive. I recommended a friend for one on one therapy because the young male had issues with female authority. After our final hour long session it was time to go.

As we were walking out my phone rang. "Hello"
"Hey it's me" he said
"Me who" I asked puzzled as I was straining to hear him.
"Malcolm" I motioned for Julian to give me a minute.
"Yes?" I said annoyed
"Can I see the baby?" he asked
"Look the last time I let you..." before I could finished he interrupted
"I'm sorry but I know Alonzo is seeing someone else and thought."
"Call me Friday and I will see if we can meet somewhere." I said
"Thank you Alisha." I locked up and walked to the car.
"Is everything alright?" Julian asked
"We will talk about it later okay." I sighed
"Okay" Julian started driving and within minutes Millie was asleep. "Babe who was that on the phone?" he asked

I looked back to check on Millie "It was Malcolm he wants to see her."

"Hell no! If he wants to see her he needs to get a court order." I was surprised to see Julian respond like that but the look on his face was serious.

"Okay Daddy J" I said and we laughed

"I did get a little upset didn't I." he laugh. "But his wife pissed me off today."

"That's understandable." I wanted to change the subject because he was going through it himself so I asked, "Have you seen your kids lately?"

"No she is fighting me tooth and nail but a decision comes out tomorrow."

"Is the divorce still final since all this mess came up?"

"Don't worry your vow to never date married or an unavailable man is still good." He laughed

"But you didn't give me a yes or no answer." I said folding my arms

"Yes we are still divorced we are just fighting over my rights as the father for visitation." He said glancing at me from the corner of his eye.

"Alright I pray all goes well." I sighed

"Pray now Alisha." I started praying and didn't stop even when his phone rung.

"Hello" Julian started smiling so stopped praying and started smiling.

When we pulled up in my driveway I got out of the car. I picked Millie up and she opened her eyes and said, "Hi mommy" before closing her eyes. I carried her into the house and took Millie upstairs to change her. When we came back down I put her in the play pen and started dinner. Julian came running in when I was almost done. "Alisha baby guess what?" he said full of excitement

"Now you know I hate that." I smiled

"That was my mom the kids will be with her until the weekend and so will..." Julian realized he had made plans with me, "I'm sorry but you know how I feel about my kids."

"Julian, you don't have to apologize be the man you are and go spend this time with your kids." I said waving him off

"I'll call you everyday" he said as he ran out the door.

That night I went to bed thinking I'm alone again and I'm trying to force something to be that is not. As I lay there my thoughts drifted to the fact that I was in my thirties and still single. I had a wonderful and successful life but I wanted a mate to share it with. I never thought this would be my desire but now I'm not sure who I love. For years men have asked me to marry them but I haven't gotten married yet. Lord, guide me because I am in a place where I am willing to settle. I closed my eyes and pushed away my pain as I fell asleep. Fifteen minutes later my phone rang. "Hello"

"Hey Alisha I hope I didn't wake you this is Blair." He said softly

"Yes you did." I said a little annoyed. I thought why was this dude calling me, when it hit me. I thought flesh you are funny I loved sex with my sexually aware teacher at one time but I am not getting mixed up with Blair Macintyre again because I am sure he is still married to some psycho.

"Sorry I was just calling to see if you wanted to meet this weekend for dinner." He said nervously

"I'm sleep call me tomorrow." I said knowing I was going to block his number.

"Okay talk to you later and it's my..." before he could finish I hung up and the phone rang again

"Hello" I said in a not so pleasant tone

"Baby are you alright?" he said

"Yes I'm just tired and my phone keeps ringing...wait, who is this?" I thought it was Julian

"It's me Alonzo, baby I had to hear your voice. I miss you, video conference me I want to see you." He said impatiently.

"What do you want Alonzo?" I said

"Is Malcolm trying to get close to you again?" he asked

"Where did...that not your concern anymore." I said

"It must be I just got some pictures of him playing with Millie and kissing you in the park." He said

"Your daughter is not spending time with him but he did call today."

"Really what did he want?" I could hear the panic in his voice

"He wants to see Millie."

"What did you say?"

"I told him to call back this weekend."

"So are you going to let him see her?"

"I don't know because I don't have a support system anymore and I wasn't thinking straight."

"Baby I will always be there for you and Millie."

I thought about how he hurt me "I really don't want to talk about this and please don't call me."

"Alisha, please don't shut me out"

"No Alonzo you hurt me good-bye" I hung up before he could respond. I was so upset with him because I held him to a higher standard but he felt his actions were excusable and to punish me for things I never did was reasonable. I was tired and then the thought of Blair calling me was crazy. That is it I'm not settling for a man so God's will and that leap Ma Carrie talked about is my desire.

I awake that morning worked out and prepared breakfast before getting ready. After I feed Millie I got her ready and we were out the door by eight. This was my daily routine. When I arrived at the clinic Rafael, the son of Mrs. Steinberg, was leaving her house. "Hi Alisha"
"Hey Rafael, how's your mom?"
"She's better and she said she wants you to come and visit."
"I will try to make it today. What happened?"
"She was a little dizzy and fainted."
"So when is she coming home?"
"She's not." He said with a sad tone
"Why?"
"Mom is going to live with Chloe and me."
"Does your mom know that?" I smiled to lighten up his mood.
"No I haven't told her yet." We both laughed as we said our good-byes.
Mrs. Steinberg was stubborn and refused to give up her house unless in her words, "They were carrying my dead body out".
Rafael was a few years younger than me

and I was like a big sister to him and his sister. I introduced him to his wife, Chloe. The three of us hung out all the time until I met her mother and she recommended to her daughter that our friendship should end.

My first appointment wasn't until eleven but when I walked up there was a woman sitting on the porch. "Hello I'm Dr. Coleman how can I help you?" I asked as I stepped onto the porch extending my hand. "Hello I'm Sarah Daniels and I'm here for the nanny interview." I had completely forgotten about the interviews. "Come in Ms. Daniels and have a seat."
"Let me give you a hand." We walked in. As I set everything up she watched Millie. Millie ran into the room to play as she held Ms. Daniels hand. I was impressed because when I walked in they were having tea. "Ms. Daniels I'm ready."
"Okay" she sighed as she got up from the tiny table.
"No mommy tea." Millie wanted to keep playing.
"Okay Millie but I need to speak with Ms. Daniels first?"
"Okay mommy" she said as she ran over and gave me a cup of tea.
"Ms. Daniels come with me" she followed

me to my office and gave me her résumé.
We talked on and off between checking on
Millie for about an hour and I wanted to
hire her on the spot but I had three more
nannies to see. We shook hands and she
departed. I texted Julian to let him know
how I felt about Ms. Daniels and he had
already done a background check on each
applicant and had an investigator to check
them out. At ten the next applicant came
but the interview was short and rigid
needless to say she was not going to get
hired.

After my first client the next nanny
appeared so I took her in the room with
Millie "Dr. Coleman I don't play with the
children." I shook her hand and escorted
her to the door. The fourth nanny was
twenty minutes late and showed up with
her child. They made it easy for me to pick
Ms. Daniels. Ms. Daniels is a widow and
retired teacher that moved here two years
ago to help her daughter after she got a
divorced so she was willing to move into the
basement apartment.

I had two clients that day and four
interviews so by three we were ready to go
home. On the way home Malcolm called me
and I ignored the call. Julian called me
later that evening. "Alisha I miss you and I

want to spend some time with you this weekend."

"Okay Julian." I said smiling.

"I planned a weekend at Manantial Spa and Resort."

"That's great but what about Millie and your kids?"

"She can come with us or you can let her spend the weekend with Alonzo's parents." He never said anything about his kids so I let it go.

"I'll think about letting her go over there. Love you talk to you later."

Julian thought I should let Millie continue to spend the weekend with Alonzo parents and I knew I should but I was hurt and angry by what his mom had done. Later that day Alonzo text me so he could video talk with Millie. "Come on Millie let's go talk to daddy." She started running and calling his name. I logged on and they spent the next five minutes talking. "Hi Alonzo it's time for Millie to eat dinner."

"Alisha my mom wants to pick Millie up on Thursday and bring her home on Sunday."

"Alonzo, I know you're doing this because of Malcolm but I would not hurt you by letting him see her if you say no. If this will make you comfortable I will let her go to your mom's house."

"Thanks Alisha. Baby I feel powerless over here without you guys."

"Alonzo you lost me not your child."

"But I lost my family when I lost you."

"I have to go." Before I could log off I heard him say he loved me. I took Millie in the kitchen to eat. After we finished dinner we played until she became sleepy. I gave her a bath and read her a story until she fell asleep. I got ready for bed and fell asleep reading.

I searched for my ringing phone with my eyes closed and answered with a sleeping voice. "Hello"

"Alisha this is Malcolm are you going to let me see the baby?"

"Malcolm her daddy does not agree with you spending time with her."

"Alisha, come on after everything he's done and I'm her father."

"Your wife came by my office and threated me so I don't trust you."

"My wife I don't have a wife?"

"Well the woman you were married to while we were sleeping together."

"What, I haven't talked to her since we got a divorce."

"She made a fake appointment to let me know you were going to take Millie."

"I would never do that all I want to do is

meet and get to know her."

"I talked to Alonzo, he was upset about it and I don't trust you."

"I'm sorry I just wanted to break you up so I could get you back but now I just want to start over with you."

"Malcolm I'll think about it."

"That's all I wanted good night."

"Wait where are these pictures coming from?"

"What pictures?"

"The one's of us kissing and of you playing with Millie."

"Letha made those she's pretty good isn't she." He laughed

"Is your wife following us?"

"Look I don't know what she's doing I just got the pictures and told her that I had not seen you but she said she got them from her Private Investigator."

"Look I don't have the energy to deal with mess."

"Alisha it's not me and I would like to put a stop to her mess but I avoid her."

"If you say so Malcolm," I sighed.

"Just think about it because I'm a changed man and I am single now." He hung up and I rolled over to continue my sleep.

Thursday evening Mr. Avery came over to pick up Millie so I meditated and wrote in my journal. Julian text he would see me Sunday so we texted back and forth for a few minutes. I sat on the sofa while I was writing in my journal and fell asleep.

Friday I got up and began my usual routine of prayer, quiet time, a good workout, and a liquid breakfast. Today I didn't know what to do with myself without Millie so I crashed on the sofa and fell asleep reading and listening to the TV. The doorbell woke me up so I jumped up and ran to the door. When I opened the door I looked into his eyes and just like Ma Carrie said my heart leapt as if we connected on another level.

Husband

I looked into my husband's eyes as he got down on one knee. "Alisha will you marry me?"
"Yes baby yes I will." He stood up and hugged me as I was shaking and crying "I never thou..."
"Come on baby pack so I can marry you."
"What do you mean marry me?"
"Just go pack because we have a few stops to make before we get there." I ran upstairs to pack and didn't know what to do so I ran in circles until he came upstairs. He grabbed me and held me tight while he gently kissed my forehead. "What should I pack?"
"A toothbrush" he laughed "just two nice outfits and keep on your sweats."
"Okay" I grabbed some underclothes my toothbrush and some comfortable clothing. We went to a lawyer's office to sign some papers and then headed to our destination.

I reclined in my seat during the ride. "Alisha what did you mean by you never thought."

"What are you talking about?"

"When I asked you to marry me you said you never thought?"

"Oh I was saying I never thought it would be you that caused my heart to leap."

"What?"

"Ma Carrie told me when I meet my husband my heart would leap like John did in Martha's belly when she saw a pregnant Mary causing John to leap in the presence of Jesus. When I looked into your eyes my heart leapt and I knew you were my husband."

"That's funny as I was talking to God while I was driving I asked Him to guide me to my wife. That night I overheard prayers from the most important people in my life asking God to send me a wife; which caused me to ponder my earlier thoughts. That night I asked God to reveal my mate before I fell asleep and dreamed of you. They were so vivid that I woke up looking for you." He chuckled "That's the ring I bought you but never placed on your finger."

"I guess God knew it was not time until today." I lay back and smiled as I thought about being the wife of the man God chose for me. "When are we going to make the announcement, start planning, and set the date for our big day?"

"Baby let's just enjoy the day" He shook his head. "You and your obsessive need to write your plans down."

"Okay but God said write it down and make it a plan; I mean plain because he guides our feet." I smiled

"That's why I can love you unconditionally." He cut on some music and held my hand until we reached our destination.

When we got to the Spa he jumped out of the car and grabbed the bags. When I opened the door to get out of the car he yelled, "Get back in the car" I got back in the car and waited for him to come back. While I was waiting I called Ma Carrie.

"Hello"

"Hi Ma Carrie its Alisha"

"Hey baby how are you?"

"I'm good but I'm engaged because my heart leapt when I saw him and then he proposed I never thought he would be the one"

"Baby only God knows who, when, why and for how long."

"Ma Carrie I love you and I will call you tomorrow."

"Alisha, keep your legs closed until you say I do or you will curse what God has blessed."

"Yes ma'am." We said our good-bye's and hung up.

Julian walked back to the car with a big smile. "Hey babe I want to go to the boutique and let you look at dresses." When we pulled up to the Manantial Wedding Boutique I said "Julian I can't go in looking like this"

"Babe didn't I say keep your sweats on, well they are expecting you."

"Why are we getting a dress when we haven't even picked a date."

"Alisha, just follow my lead because this is how I wanted to do it with you years ago."

"Ok I will not ask another question and allow you to fulfill your dream." We got out and walked in to an awaiting staff. One woman took me to look at dresses and I was surprised to see they were a soft pink and then I saw the dress of my dreams. It was strapless and plain and fitted down to the waist and slightly flared out to the floor into a train in the back. After I picked out the dress she showed me some shoes which were an easy choice as was the veil. She rushed me back to Julian. "Are you ready to go Alisha?"

"Whenever you are Julian," I said smiling. "Let's get the full service before we go back to the room."

"That sounds good to me but can we do it after we eat?"

"Just a light snack because you're getting a full massage and makeover." When we got back I followed the lady back for a full massage and then a total make over we were not done until eight that evening. We got the car and headed to our room. Julian opened the door "Alisha, get dressed for dinner." I walked into my room and there was an attendant in there. "Hello Mrs. Coleman I'm here to assist you with getting dressed." I thought Julian really wanted to enjoy this weekend. "Have your way with me" I took a shower and she helped me get dressed. There was a knock on the door "Babe, are you ready we are going to eat in the back so I'll be outside waiting on you." I walked out and his father met me at the door "Hello Mr. Carothers I didn't know you would be joining us." When we walked out the door leading to the garden music begin to play. I looked at his father and thought is this what I think is yes I had on my dress but...When I looked up Julian had a big smile so I started to cry. This was my wedding and he planned everything and got what I wanted from the color to the place. When I reached him I saw tears of joy as he kissed my hand. The Preacher started with a prayer and begun reading the vows.

"Julian Carothers do you take Alisha Coleman to be…" Julian placed the ring on my finger as did I when it was my turn. The Preacher announced us we kissed and had our first dance as husband and wife.

That evening Julian and I explored a love that was no longer forbidden; I had never experienced that. Julian always had an issue with quickness when it came to me so he asked me to be patient with him. As we explored one another I felt different because for the first time in my life I was doing this right and the love increased my passion and desire for him. That night I lay in my husband's arms thinking how complete my life had become when I focused on the spirit instead of the flesh.

"Julian you tricked me." I said kissing his arms.

"Baby I couldn't wait another day for you to be my wife" I kissed Julian as his embrace became tighter. "All those years I longed for you so when my wife started cheating with Carlton I didn't care because I wanted to be with you antway."

"You said you wanted her back"

"I will always love the mother of my children but I wanted to spend the rest of my life with a woman I couldn't have."

"What do you mean?"

"You pushed me away back then so I tested you this time to see if I could have you." "Julian I did want you but I was not mature enough for a committed relationship." I knew that wasn't the complete truth but I was not ready to tell the truth. "Yes you were but fear held you back and I am so glad you've overcome that issue." I smiled because I thought he was so self-absorbed that he would never realize the truth causing me to ponder if I was just as self-centered. He told me since the day he came to my house and found out that I was single he planned to marry me. "Alisha I was not going to miss out on you being my wife again." Julian caressed me with his tongue until he reached my burning desire for him as he pulled my legs further apart I moaned and arched my back from uncontrollable pleasure as I grabbed Julian's head to force him deeper into my burning sweetness for him I released my essence. I slightly rose from the bed and Julian slowly entered my essence drenched passion as the warmth of my essence surrounded his penetrating desire for me. With each stroke he struggle holding back the fullness of his essence but within minutes he cursed as pulled out but gave in to the sudden release he longed for. Julian was not done he kissed me and returned to the sweetness of his desire and caressed the juices with his tongue until I was fully engulfed with his pleasure as he wrapped his arms around my thighs to give himself full control of my swaying hips. With the arch of my back I gave myself to him as I exploded he enjoyed every drop of me causing me to squeeze his head tighter as I cried out in pleasure. Julian kissed my forehead and we drifted off to sleep.

The next morning I slept later than usual and didn't awake until Julian brought me breakfast in bed.
"Good morning, my beautiful wife." He smiled.
I thought it was a dream until I looked at him and then my hand. Tears of joy fell from my eyes so I said "Good morning my love." I caressed his face as I sat up. He had my favorite Banana Foster's French toast and Mimosa with sprite and orange juice. I found out later the Mimosa was real so we could toast our new life, I took two sips and he gave me my virgin Mimosa. "So, what is Millie going to call me?"
"What do you want her to call you?"
"She can call me Poppa or Daddy J."
"Poppa no and Daddy may hurt Alonzo."
"Well she can't call me Julian or what she calls me now."

"What does she call you?"

"Nothing you haven't said my name in front of her since we decided to date."

"I haven't."

"No it's always him or nothing."

"I can't believe I've done that, why didn't you say something?"

"It wasn't a big deal I knew it hard for you dealing with the break-up."

"Baby, forgive me for being so insensitive." I said as I leaned over and kissed him.

"It didn't bother me because I knew you were mine."

"Oh really mister cocky"

"You should know better than I do." He laughed as he removed my tray and spread my legs apart. Julian was engulfed with the warmth of his sweetness he whispered in my ear, "I've been waiting on this for such a long time I've missed the warm juicy softness of you; oh baby I can't" he said as he released his essence I eased from under him to take a shower. A few minutes later he walked into the shower. I turned and began to wash my husband's well chiseled body. After I soaped him up I placed him under the waterfall of the shower and as the suds were washed away I dropped down and caressed the love he had just given me with my tongue as I swirled my tongue around his throbbing desire he grabbed my head and thrust himself as far as he could down my throat as he retreated like a vacuum I caused him to return with more force until he fell back on the shower wall releasing my reward. "Shit what the fu...." Julian slid down the wall as I took control and mounted my mocha love he continue to moan in pleasure he gripped my behind tighter which cause my thrust to become harder and faster until we both gave up our essence. I kissed Julian on the nose. "Baby you are lasting a lot longer."

"I know I was concentrating and you are going to kill me." He laughed "You have the same drive but it's warmer and wetter than when I first met you. Shit woman you are not going to kill a brother by giving it to me like that."

"Come on Julian you know I won't kill you well I'll try not to." I laughed and we got up and finished our shower. Julian got out first so when I walked into the bed room he ushered me to the bed. He laid me on my back at the edge of the bed as my legs rose he licked every part of me. I lay there enjoying every moment as he explored every part of his wife, until I was completely exhausted. Julian pulled me to my feet and turned me around and he bent me over, Malcolm flashed into my mind, as he slowly entered me I gripped his hand that rested on my stomach and he added more lubricant. After he was completely engulfed he lost himself after seven or eight thrust giving up his essence. "Damn baby I can't control myself with you anywhere." He fell on the bed breathing hard as I lay next to him he kissed me. "Alisha! Who popped your cherry?"

"What?" I knew what he was asking me but I was so ashamed that I had given Malcolm every part of me because he was the man who had my mind and drove my sexual lust.

Julian rose up off the bed as he said in anger, "Who fucked you in..."

Before he could finish I yelled "Malcolm."

"Is that Milagro's real father?"

"Yes, are you upset?"

"No I just wanted to be your first something." He fell back on the bed and I sat there thinking of everything I had given up because I refused to let go of the hurt from that one summer day and settled for less.

Julian pulled me down next to him. "Baby I know you had a life before and after me before we got married. It's not you I'm upset with I should've left Rasheda and stayed with you but you wouldn't let me get close to you so I gave up." He pulled me closer "After everything I went through with her I couldn't take you leaving me for another man and I thought she would be faithful. The day I saw you with Thomas I was jealous but relieved to find out that you were just friends. I wanted what he wanted but couldn't have it so we settled for your friendship."

"Julian I'm sorry because before Malcolm I was afraid to let my guard down and I missed out on so many special and beautiful moments in my life because I couldn't let go of what happened to me that summer day."

"Baby what happened?" I looked a Julian and told him my deepest darkest secret. I told him the events of that summer day. As I talked tears flowed but my voice was steady and strong. The more I talked and with each tear drop I felt renewed and restored. After I finished Julian sat there in shocked but the look on his face was rage.

"Julian, are you alright?" I asked shaking him.

"How could anyone do that?" He shook his head and tears appeared but never fell.

"Alisha I will never hurt you intentionally and if I do please tell me." I smiled and kissed my husband.

"Let's get ready for lunch." I ran into the bathroom to take a shower and when I looked up Julian looked as if he was scared to come in. "Julian, honey is everything alright?"

"Yes I was thinking do you know where any of those people are or remember their names?"

"The past is the past and it's over."

"But they hurt you."

"Julian if that day would not have happened I wouldn't be standing in the shower waiting on you right now, my first husband." I said with a sly grin as I leaned back on the shower wall and opened my legs. Julian ran into the shower and tasted his wife until I cried out releasing my passion fulfilled essence to him. Julian turned around to shower as I assisted him I reminisced about the pleasure he had given me. Julian picked me up and lost his throbbing manhood into the warmth of my pleasure as he thrust harder and harder we fell back onto the shower wall and I cried out in total pleasure Julian whispered in my ear, "This pussy is so damn good," with his final trust he gave himself up to me. I finished with my shower and went into the bedroom to get dressed. Julian walked in and asked, "Alisha can you get pregnant?"

"What?"

"Are you on the pill?"

"No why."

"Is it cool for us to have a baby now?"

"Julian...oh crap I just thought about what you were saying."

"So are you ready?"

"If I get pregnant than we will have a baby but are you ready?"

"Yes." He walked over and picked me up. "Julian, what made you think about that?"

"When I met you we used condoms all the time and you were on the pill but I haven't seen any pills and we haven't used a condom yet."

"We used condoms for protection from STD's and since we've been tested and monogamous there is no need for condoms. I've been trying to stop having sex so I've been off the pill for years."

"Is that how you got Millie the condom broke?"

"No that's a different story."

"You can tell me on the way to the café for lunch." As we walked to the café I told him about my time with Malcolm and the sordid details. After I finished Julian stopped and looked at me, "And this punk wants to make demands on seeing our Millie."

"Julian it's the past and we can't live there but we can use it to learn and grow."

"I know but the more I hear about this guy the less I like him."

"Come on Julian lets go in."

As we walked into the café a group of women were standing together. One of the ladies walked extremely close to Julian. After she rubbed her chest on him she said, "Hello Julian. I heard you got a divorce." She turned until she was between us and her back towards me. "This is my wife," Julian said pushing the woman over, "excuse me." Julian turned his back towards her grabbed my hand and walked towards the hostess. She led us to our table.

After we ordered I was ready to go back to the Villa so I rubbed my foot on Julian's leg and smiled. "Damn girl I told you earlier you are not going to kill me."
"Come on Julian let's get our food sent to the room."
"No we are going to eat right here and I'll give you some later." He smiled and winked at me. "I forgot about your appetite I might need to call in Thomas." He laughed as I turned up my nose and rolled my eyes. "Alisha I was just kidding." He said as he reached out for my hand and I playfully pulled it back.
"Baby, will you be able to keep up with me?"
"Yeah girl I was just joking but you already bought it so if you break it you can't get

anymore." We laughed and continued our conversation which included our living arrangements, kids, and work. "I have it Julian she can call you DJ short for Daddy Julian."

"DJ I like that so what about your last name?"

"I will change it." The waitress came over and he signed the receipt as we got up he placed a tip on the table.

We walked to the lake before going back to our room. "I want to take you right now," I said. Julian pulled me closer to him and kissed my forehead because children were playing nearby. After he kissed me I took off running back to our villa. Julian caught me before I got to the door and carried me over the threshold. "Did you know I love my wife?"

"Did you know I love my husband?" Julian pulled up my short summer dress and kissed my warm passion as I moaned he carried me to the bed. Julian pulled down my panties and embraced my burning pleasure that was unquenchable. As I spread my legs for him to embrace my passion I rose up from the bed to enjoy the view of his work causing me to grab his head as I thrust my hip to meet his love I exploded in ecstasy. I pulled him down on the bed and with perfect balance I glided up and down on the tip of his throbbing love when he would assist I would stop causing him to cry out for more of the warmth he desired. Each cry would cause me to slide further and further into his pleasure until he grabbed a hold of me squeezing me tighter thrusting into the warm wetness until he exploded. Julian convulsed and squeezed me until he lost all strength. Julian had superb tongue action which made me hunger for more but he rolled over and went to sleep. I got up to call Ma Carrie to tell her the good news.

"Hello"

"Hi Ma Carrie I called to let you know I'm married."

"Child you just called me yesterday you couldn't keep your legs closed?"

"No he surprise with a wedding when I got here. As soon as he proposed he whisked me off and had everything set up."

"Is he saved?"

"Yes ma'am he is. I've known him for several years and Tommy knows him too. I've even known his family and he treats his mother and daughter right."

"Well I guess we taught you something" She laughed. "I give my blessings to you and him."

"Love you Ma Carrie." I said. After we hung

up I pulled up Tommy's number but I had an incoming call from Mr. Avery. "Hello"

"We're bringing Millie home today after she's released."

"Why are you bringing her home...wait released; released from where?"

"Millie was running a fever last night so we took her to the emergency room and they admitted her."

"Wait you took her to the ER and didn't call me"

"I thought she called you but I guess it was Alonzo. She told him she couldn't reach you but left a message."

"Thank you Mr. Avery I will see you in a couple of hours."

"We are still at the hospital."

"Thanks again Mr. Avery." After I got off the phone I woke Julian up. "Julian we have to go"

Julian was groggy so he rubbed his eyes saying, "Baby what?"

"We need to leave Millie was taken to the ER." Julian jumped up and helped me get our stuff packed so we could leave. It took us less than five minutes to get everything up and to the car. "Which hospital did they her to?"

"Children's First," I said covering my face to pray.

"Let me make a phone call and we'll find

out what going on." Julian called his mother and she called back within twenty minutes. Millie had been to the ER twice and they had just admitted her today. She had a fever and was dehydrated from throwing up and the doctors couldn't find out what was wrong because she was better when she went home but came back later that day with the same symptoms. I started crying and blamed myself for letting her go over there. Julian looked at me and said angrily "Alisha those are her grandparents they would not hurt her."

"It's not them I'm worried about its Alonzo's girlfriend I don't want her around my baby."

"Why?"

"Julian have you ever had that feeling in the pit of your stomach about somebody but you couldn't put your finger on it."

"Yes plenty of times during business deals."

"Well that's how I feel about her."

"Are you sure it's not jealousy?"

"Yes, I'm a big girl so I can deal with him moving on."

"Alisha this man took on a big commitment and adopted Millie because he loved you. I take my hat off to him so if you are upset that's understandable."

"Yes I was upset because he just gave up on us."

"So, that made you jealous of his girlfriend."

"No it's not her it's what his mother is trying to do."

"What is she doing?"

"Trying to make them a family and push me out."

"But you are not a family."

"I mean pull Millie away from me and get her closer to Ginger."

"Okay I get it now. I see why you don't want her over there." I smiled at Julian with water covered eyes as we rode in silence he held my hand.

The honeymoon was over and real life was about to begin.

Payback

We were at the hospital in less than two hours and we went directly to her room. "Excuse me Ms. you are not allowed up here unless you're family"
"I am the mother of Milagro Vida Coleman-Avery and this is my husband"
"I'm sorry but her mother is already..."
"Her what?" I shouted becoming enraged.
"Baby I have it just calm down." Julian grabbed me by my arm and pulled me away as he pulled out his phone and talked for what seemed like two minutes. The nurse received a phone call and was apologizing as security was coming through the door. The nurse rushed us into the room. The Avery's were sitting down as Ginger stood over Millie. "Get out" I said in a low growl as I squinted my eyes. Ginger yelled. "I'm her mother because we couldn't find you so I'm not leaving." I turned towards security and they walked over to Ginger, "Ma'am you must leave." Ginger snatched away as I walked over to Millie tears ran down my

face and Ginger pushed me but all I could focus on was Millie until she slapped me. That caused me to snap back into reality and Julian ran over to me as security handcuffed Ginger and dragged her out. "No don't hurt her she was only protecting her child." Mrs. Avery exclaimed as she ran after them. Mr. Avery walked over to me with tears and shacking his head, "I'm sorry Alisha."

I hugged Mr. Avery "This has nothing to do with you so keep in touch." He walked out. Julian talked with the nurse and gave her the names of the three people who could visit Millie. As I held my baby girls hand through the crib I prayed and tears fell. Julian came back into the room and stood behind me as I prayed he held me tighter and he begin to pray.

I fell asleep standing up banging my head on the rail of the crib every time I dosed off as Julian slept in the chair. The next morning I heard "Mommy Mommy" Millie jumped up and kissed me. I was so excited I picked her up out of the crib and almost snatched the needle out of her foot. The doctors were making their rounds and when he walked into the room he was surprised to see her up. "Good morning little one" the Doctor turned to me and asked "Where is her mother and grandparents?"

"I am her mother and her grandparents went home."

The confused and questioning look on his face retired as he spoke "We could not find anything wrong with her and as you can see she's back to her normal self."

"Will she be well enough to come home soon?"

"We will draw more blood this morning but if the results come back clean and she is active by noon she can leave today."

"Thank you" the doctor left and a few minutes later the lab came in to draw her blood.

I reached for my phone to call Mr. Avery and couldn't find it. "Julian did I have my phone last night?"

"I'm not sure but I'll go check the car."

Julian came back in with my phone a few minutes later "It was on the charger."

"Thanks baby." I looked at my phone and I had text messages and voice mails galore. "I forgot to call Alonzo" I dialed his number and the call went to voice mail so I called back. "What the hell is wrong with you, when did you become so evil?"

"What are you talking about?"

"You had my mom kicked out of the

hospital and arrested"

"No I didn't but she did leave out behind Ginger."

"Whatever how is Millie?"

"She's better and she may come home today."

"That's good no thanks to you." I walked into the patient's bathroom.

"What are you talking about?"

"My mom couldn't find you so she asked me to see if it would be alright if Ginger helped out with Millie.

"She couldn't find me, your mother never called me your dad did."

"He would make excuses for you because he was the same way missing when my mother needed him."

"I came as soon as I found out from your dad and he only called once he realized your mother never called me."

"Look Alisha I know you don't like my mom but I will get her to file for legal rights to see Millie."

"Okay Alonzo, do what you have to do."

"Were you with a man?"

"Yes I was."

"You're a bitch my mom was right about you." I hung up the phone as I walked out of the bathroom. "Are you alright Alisha?"

"Yes Julian I don't know what his mother and Ginger told him but he called me a bitch. Alonzo is not the type of man to say that about a woman." I whispered to Julian after he kissed my forehead I walked to Millie's bedside "Daddy said hi and he is glad you're better"

"Talk to Daddy" I pulled out my phone and called Alonzo but the phone went to voice mail so I called again and this time I let her leave a message. Julian could see I still loved Alonzo and was a bit saddened by the revelation.

At one o'clock the nurse came in with the discharge papers and we took Millie home. I ran upstairs to shower and change while she slept. Julian went home and packed. He was selling the house he bought with Rasheda. He had moved back into the house on his parent's estate. After I got out of the shower I called Mr. Avery again to see if he wanted to set up Fridays to spend time with Millie.

Julian moved in and our family life was looking brighter but the relationship between Alonzo and I was a disaster. He talked to Millie every day on video chat and we only talked with a text when he wanted to talk to her. I let Julian know I would be spending Friday's with Mr. Avery and Millie so he was in agreement with that. Mr. Avery and I became close after a month of spending time with each other. Alonzo chatted with Millie were twice a week now and she never went to see his mother. The first petition was shot down because we had a better lawyer. Mr. Avery testified that he saw Millie whenever he wanted but Elaine, Mrs. Avery, would never call to check on her or ask to visit. The story told to Alonzo was different so he was coming home in a month to handle everything but he never came.

During my talks with Mr. Avery on Friday's I found out that Mrs. Avery never called me the day Millie went to the hospital. Alonzo never believe his dad because they were never close because of the way he neglected his mom. Alonzo was the love child of a fling that Mrs. Avery had with Mr. Avery's pool buddy Eddie. He introduced Mildred to Eddie and they hit it off the first night and Mrs. Avery was jealous. Mr. Avery worked a lot because she wanted to live a lavished lifestyle and she never loved him just what he had to offer. She was in love with fast talking lady loving Eddie her best friend's boyfriend and her husband's friend. She would have him come over while the kids were in school. When she realized she was pregnant she told Eddie and he disappeared. She had not been having sex with Mr. Avery but he knew she was pregnant before she did so he played along. After that he started having an affair with her best friend Mildred, who was Eddie's girlfriend. After he filed for divorce he confronted her when she brought Alonzo home. He put her out because the divorce was final by that time but he missed the kids and let her come back. She hated him after that because he never remarried or slept in the same room with her again. She didn't know that Ginger was Mr. Avery's daughter and Mildred was the reason he let her come back and never had sex with her again. Ginger and Mildred would go on all the family trips. That's why he was missing in action because he spent most of his time at work or with his child and the woman he loved.

Julian and I had settled in good as a family except for his choice to be a pilot. His mom and I agreed that he should not do it but his father encouraged him. A few months after the dust had settled Julian, Millie and I were sitting in the family room when the doorbell rang. He got up to answer the door and started yelling, "Alisha, Alisha baby you have to see this" I jumped up grabbing Millie as I walked towards the door and screamed, "Tommy" I put Millie down and ran towards him jumping in his arms. "Okay Alisha, this better be the only time you jump in another man's arms." I was so excited I didn't see the beautiful woman standing next to him. "Tommy when did you…why…okay let me calm down so we can go in the family room to talk."

"Wait Alisha I would like for you to meet my fiancée Isabella Esperanza Santiago"

"Hello Isabella how are you?"

"Hello Ilesha nice to finally meet you." She stuck out her hand

"No its Alisha but I call her Lisha" Tommy said as he grabbed her around the waist and stuck his tongue in her mouth. Julian and I looked at each other in surprise because that was not the conservative Tommy or Thomas we knew. By the time they finished we I had put Millie in the playpen and had walked back to the door. "Well alrighty then would you guys like to freshen up?" I asked

"Yes could you show her to the room while I see my god-daughter."

I took her to one of the main level bedrooms while Julian walked with Tommy into the family room. "Hey Tommy's baby" He said as he picked up Millie and she squealed "Tom Tom" they played for a while.

"Hey Julian what are you doing here?"

"Alisha didn't tell you?"

"Tell me what?"

I walked into the room saying, "That we got married."

"Hell no. Why didn't you call me?"

"I did but your voicemail was full and if you had called to tell me you were coming or engaged I could've been prepared for you."

"Alisha it happened so fast that we came home sooner than expected."

Isabella walked over to Tommy "Yes Thomas and I had to leave when people found out about our relationship." She looked at me "Alisha why do you call him Tommy when everyone else calls him Thomas?"

"Ma Carrie and I have always called him that."

"Well I don't like it and you should stop." She said stomping her foot

"Natasha I mean Isabella...."

Tommy spoke up before I could finish.

"Baby we are just friends"

"Well I don't like her and I think we should leave because she wants you."

I shook my head in disbelief, "Not again Tom... I mean Thomas."

He pulled me to the side "Come on Alisha you didn't want me and I deserve to be happy."

"Yes you do but don't come crying to me

this time."

Julian felt uncomfortable and asked, "Would any one like a drink?"

"Yes I brought this you know how I like it and make it a double." Tommy said.

"I would like the same as Thomas" Julian said with a hearty laugh holding up the bottle.

"I'll take Millie upstairs and get her ready for bed." I said annoyed.

By the time I came down Isabella was feeling good and flirty. They had cut on music and she was dancing in front of Julian so he got up, "Thomas get your girl because I have a happy home and I am going to keep it that way."

"She's just dancing Julian." He laughed.

"Alisha wont trip like that." Julian moved and sat in one of the chairs on the opposite side of the room but Isabella came over and straddled him. Julian jumped up and yelled, "Get the fuck off of me I just told you to stay away from me." He looked at her in disgust. "You are not going to keep disrespecting my wife." I walked in while Julian was yelling, "Thomas you can stay but she's got to go." Julian walked out and went upstairs.

"What's going on Tommy?" I asked puzzled.

"Isabella was dancing in front of Julian but he thought she was disrespecting you."

"And you didn't?"

"She was just dancing but we'll leave in the morning." Tommy said puzzled.

"You don't have to go." I said reassuring him. I knew they were a little tipsy.

"Yes I do because I'm taking her home tomorrow." Tommy slurred.

"To Ma Carrie?" I said looking at him as if he lost his mind.

"Yes and the rest of the family, do you have a problem with that?"

"No Tommy this is your life to live and you only answer to God."

"But God wouldn't give me you."

"Did you ever think it was a purpose for that?"

"No I just wanted you."

"But we were not ready and we still have something most people could never have and that's an everlasting bond. Tommy I will always love my best friend." Tommy kissed me on the forehead and went to bed.

When I got upstairs Julian was still pissed, "Baby can you believe that woman and how is it that Thomas can't see her for what she is?"

"Baby we all have our flaws."

"But Thomas is a good guy he deserves better."

"I know."

"Baby, have you and Thomas ever dated?"

"No we haven't."

"Has he ever had you?"

"What made you ask me that?"

"It was the way he looked at you when she said you wanted him and I know he was in love with you."

"Yes, after well before you"

"Then why are you not with him?"

"Because unlike you he didn't make my heart leap and I never felt that way about him."

"But I know he's in love with you and you love him."

"We were together twice because we were both hurt and comforted one another the wrong way but we are not meant to be."

"I trust you and I have never trusted a woman so you can be friends."

"Why did you feel the need to tell me that?"

"Because I trust your friendship with Thomas and if you guys need some time alone to talk I'm okay with that."

I leaned over and kissed Julian, "I love you and there is not a man on this earth that is worth my breaking that trust or our bond." Julian slid over and started kissing me "I'm glad God gave you to me because that benefit between your legs will cause any man to lose his mind." Julian eased off my sweats and buried his head between my legs as I moaned in pleasure we heard a loud noise coming from down stairs. Julian jumped up, "Hell no if they are fighting they are leaving tonight." He ran down stairs but returned quicker than he departed. "What's wrong Julian?"

"Now I see why she acts like that."

"What happened?"

"I am not telling you because dude made me feel bad." I jumped up to go down stairs and Julian grabbed me by my arm. "Baby he is down there doing her like he lost his mind."

"Julian, are they having sex?"

"Yes"

"I thought they were fighting" I pulled my pants down. "Now you get back to work." Julian pulled me over his face. It was as if he never stopped but I could hear the screams of Isabella and they became distracting so I slide down and embraced his love with my tongue before engulfing it with my mouth causing him to grab my head and force himself deeper exploding with incoherent words and spasms. I rested on his face again until I erupted with pleasure. Julian pulled me closer and fell asleep I lay in bed with a burning desire that he never quenched. A few hours later I felt his tongue caressing my longing and I moaned as he pulled me to the edge of the bed and forced his throbbing passion in as hard and quick as he could. It was as if this would be the last time he would ever feel me, after a few quick hard strokes he caressed the dripping passion I gave him causing me to release my essence as he quickly penetrated my passion with his throbbing love. For the next hour Julian did that and for the first time I slept without craving more because he didn't release after he took all I had to give. Julian had never had sex with me like that before.

I awake the next morning with Julian on top of me but I flipped him over and mounted my mocha stallion causing him to release his essence immediately. "Baby, what were you drinking last night?"
"Some stuff Thomas brought."
"Tell him to leave the bottle"
"Why?"
"You don't remember last night."
"Not really I just know I woke up with a need to get in you."
"Well last night we lasted for almost an hour."
"Alisha I went to sleep after you got off my face" he laugh
"Julian at three you got up gave me my favorite turned me over tagged me and you did that until four in the morning."

"I lasted longer than twenty minutes with you?"

"Yes so go steal that bottle from Tommy while I cook breakfast." I got up but my legs were weak so I fell. Julian ran over to help me up "Are you alright?"

"Yes," I said smiling as I looked up at him. "I'm going to steal that bottle," he said as we laughed. "Now I know why she was acting like that and he was fucking her like he lost his mind."

"Julian have you noticed how much Tommy has changed?"

"Yes but I think it's because of Isabella."

"Yeah but he acts like he threw away his belief."

"Baby people find out who they are when exposed to real life."

"I know but his last wife hurt him so bad and I'm just scared for my friend." Julian hugged me as he kissed my forehead, "I know baby."

I took a shower and Julian decided to go downstairs to talk to Tommy. When Julian walked into the kitchen he saw him on the sofa in the family room. "Hey Thomas is everything alright?"

"Hey Julian yea man, where's Alisha?"

"She's upstairs but she'll be down in a minute to start breakfast."

"Man I wanted to talk to you for a minute."

"Okay what's up?"

"First forgive my lady for disrespecting you and Alisha but she had to give up everything to be with me. She's been stressed and scared I would leave her for another woman."

"Man she's insecure?"

"No she's not and I've never seen that side of her. I know Alisha is worried about me because of my first wife but I need Isabella and Alisha to get along so can you help?"

"How long have you been knowing that head strong over protective woman?"

"I know but I was thinking about buying a house up here once I found a job."

"I can help you with a job and finding a house but after last night your girl is going to have to work on that with Alisha."

"I hope they can work it out."

"Hey what are my guys up to?" I said as I walked into the room with Millie and put her in the playpen.

Julian jumped up and ran over to me.

"Nothing baby so what are you making for breakfast?"

"I am making French Toast, eggs, ham and cutting up some fresh fruit." I said with a smile

"That's what I'm talking about my Lisha in the kitchen tearing it up." Tommy said

"Thomas I have told both of you she belongs to me." Julian said with a laugh.

I gave Julian a playful push as I twisted my mouth, "Tommy what were y'all drinking last night?"

"Aguardiente de Orujo, the first night we met Isabella gave me that to drink and I've been in heaven ever since."

"Well give Julian that bottle." I shouted from the kitchen.

"I brought two bottles for you guys and you're welcome Alisha." Julian looked at Tommy kind of strange as he walked into the kitchen. Tommy went to check on Isabella.

"What have you been telling him?" Julian whispered.

"What are you talking about." I asked puzzled.

"Have you been telling him about our sex life?" Julian was a little upset.

"No!" I exclaimed and continued cooking "Then why did he say you're welcome Alisha?"

"Because he knows your wife has an unquenchable sex drive and I'm probably killing you." I laughed.

"That shit's not funny Alisha."

I continued to set the table for breakfast as he walked out.

Julian came into the kitchen with Millie after Tommy and Isabella sat down at the table. I started putting the food on the table but before I could sit down I ran to the bathroom. Tommy jumped up before Julian but they both ran behind me. "Lisha baby are you alright?" Tommy yelled through the bathroom door. "Thomas will you move so I can see about my wife now go in there with your girl." Tommy walked back into the dining room while Julian walked into the bathroom. When Tommy got back Isabella was upset and they started to argue. Julian rubbed my back and asked, "Baby, are you alright?"

"Yes but I think you're going to be a daddy." Julian started yelling and ran into the dining room "Thomas, were going to have a baby man!" Tommy jumped up forgetting about the spat with Isabella and high fived Julian. "Are you sure we're going to have a baby?"

"Well she said I think but I knew it, I've been trying since we got married."

As I walked into the room I said, "Oh you have huh?"

"Well I told you I wanted us to build a family now."

Tommy ran over to me assisting me to my chair, "Tommy what are you doing?" I said as I pushed him away.

"Thomas leave her alone and come sit over here with me." Isabella cried.

Tommy walked over to Isabella. "Alisha did you want more children?" Isabella asked as she rubbed Millie's head. Millie was so busy eating the excitement was unnoticed until she finished her eggs. "Mommy more" Millie said as she held up her plate.

"Julian will you get here some more eggs while I go upstairs and lie down." I kissed him on the cheek. "Thanks babe."

"Alisha I'm getting a full time nanny for you."

"Julian you can do what you want. Tommy what time is your flight?"

"We leave at one but now I want to stay longer." Isabella had a look of disapproval on her face.

"No Tommy you go home. Isabella it was nice meeting you." She gave me a nod that included a fake smile.

"Alisha I'll be up to see you before I leave." Isabella stormed out and the doorbell rang. Julian went to the door as Tommy cleaned off the table. "Hello Ms. Daniels how are you?"

"Hello Julian where's my lil Miss Millie?"

"She's in the dining room eating eggs as usual." Ms. Daniels was always there by eight during her four day work week andbefore ten on the weekend if she was working but if she stayed over she prepared breakfast for everyone. She made her way to the dining room and when Millie saw her she waved frantically and shouted, "Ma D Ma D." she tried to get out of her chair as Julian walked in. "Ms. Daniels I need to talk with you about something."

"Yes Julian," she said as she reach down to pick up Millie.

"We may need to hire you full time."

"Why would you do that Julian?"

"Alisha might be pregnant so she will need extra help."

"Does she know about this conversation child?"

"Yes ma'am I told her I would talk to you."

"You told her but did she agree?"

"I know what you mean but she's not fighting me on this."

"We can sit down later and talk."

Tommy called Julian into my office. "Hey I need to talk to you about something."

"What's up Thomas?"

"I wanted to know if the bond Alisha and I have bothers you?"

"No," Julian patted him on the back. "I know everything about you and Alisha but that was before me."

"You know about us?"

"Yes I do, is that what you wanted to talk about?"

"No. Julian I love Alisha and it's important that she accepts my wife because I am going to marry Isabella once I buy a house up here and get a job."

"I understand the importance of that but Isabella that keeps disrespecting Alisha."

"I know, when I get home I'll sit her down and talk with her."

"If I didn't know both of you already I would have an issue with your friendship especially since I know you slept together."

"Julian I would never touch Alisha while she's with you and I've moved on with my life because she's meant to be my friend and that's it."

"I respect that and I trust both of you Thomas." They shook hands and Tommy went to pack the car as Julian came up to check on me. Tommy and Julian became friend's years ago so they knew how the other felt but didn't let it interfere with their relationship. The first time they met was during a lunch date I had with Tommy when he came to visit for the first time and sealed that friendship with their first golf game. At the time they both wondered if I was dating and had dated the other, but only revealed that to me years later.

Tommy came upstairs to talk with me as Julian talked to Isabella about my relationship with Tommy. "Hey Lisha, how are you feeling?"

"I'm good Tommy; are you ready to leave?" I'm packed but I wanted you and Isabella to be friends."

"Tommy because I love you I will respect and love her but after last night I don't really like her."

"She's not like that and I don't know what was wrong with her last night."

"Tommy for your sake I will give her another chance but if she hurts you I'm done; deal?"

"Deal," Tommy hugged me after he kissed me on the forehead. "I love you Alisha and you were right we are meant to only be friends." I got up to walk Tommy out but he stopped me. "You get some rest I have to see about Millie before I go."

"But Tommy I have to get up because Julian won't let me lift a finger and he is not even sure if I'm pregnant I guess it was a good thing I didn't have any appointments today."

"Well that's even more of a reason to lie back down."

"You make me sick Tommy."

"It was you doing the nasty that made you sick cause your belly is full of baby now." I playfully hit Tommy on the arm as we laughed at that old saying. Tommy went down stairs and spent his last few moment with Millie before they left for their flight.

Ms. Daniels took Millie to the park and Julian came upstairs with me. "Baby I canceled my first lesson so I could spend some time with you."
"Julian will you reconsider taking flying lessons now that I might be pregnant?"
"Pee on this stick and we will see." I took the test thinking when di he guy this test. Julian was like a kid in the candy store as we waited for the results.
When time was up Julian ran into the bathroom and started jumping up and down.
He pulled out his phone and called his mother. "I did it Alisha is pregnant"
"Have you been to the doctor yet?"
"No not yet but she will make an appointment soon."
Julian hung up the phone after the brief conversation.
Julian licked his lips and walked over to me as he spread my legs and tasted me ever so gently causing me to arch my back in pleasure while pulling his love closer to me. Once I gave him the satisfaction he was searching for. Julian turned me over but

before I could get to my knees he pushed through my burning passion with a stroke of lustful intent. Once I was stable I swirled my hips causing an eruption of passion as Julian gave me the last of himself I whispered in his ear, "get a shot of that drink tonight because I what more."

We held each other until we doze off.

Best Friend's Wife

When Tommy got home he was not welcomed by his father or mother but Ma Carrie was excited to see him and embraced Isabella. Tommy returned to his house and started packing for the new transition in his life. Tommy decided to move within two weeks whether he found a job or not because that little town was too much. Ma Carrie asked about my husband and everything he did while he had been gone. Whenever Tommy was home Ma Carrie would move in with him. Julian and I had already decided to take a trip to see Ma Carrie so we thought we could surprise Tommy as well. We flew out Friday afternoon and rented a car at the airport I called Tommy when we got close to his house. "Hello"

"Hey Tommy its Alisha, where are you?"

"At my house," he looked at the phone as if I had asked a crazy question "Lisha I think that baby is affecting you already."

"Oh shut up Tommy."

"Well Alisha it was a stupid question."
"No its not if I'm on my way to see you."
"What?"
"I think you're going deaf in your old age." I
laughed.
"What time does your flight get here?"
"It's here we are sitting outside your
house." Tommy ran out the door and
greeted us. "Where is Ma Carrie?" I asked
as Isabella came to the door
"She's in the house." I ran in to see Ma
Carrie as Tommy and Julian unloaded the
car. Isabella showed Ms. Daniels to a
bedroom as Julian carried a sleeping Millie.

I walked into the room and yelled, "Ma
Carrie" and gave her a big hug.
"Alisha baby girl let me look at you and
where is that husband of yours."
I took a step back and she looked at me
"My Julian is unloading the car."
"My my so you're pregnant too"
"Ma Carrie did Tommy tell you I was
pregnant?"
"No I can see it in your face."
"Wait you said too who else is pregnant?"
"Tommy's wife but they haven't told me yet
either" Tommy told his family that he was
married to Isabella.
"Are you sure because he hasn't said
anything to me either." I thought about the

night she drank and Tommy said she doesn't drink and her attitude had changed. "Ma Carrie, are you sure?" "Child I've been on this earth long enough to know when a woman is full of baby." I laughed. Julian walked in "I hope y'all are saying good things about me." When Ma Carrie looked up at my fine 6'2" brown eyed mocha dream with jet black hair and perfect smile she said, "Now I see why you married him hell if I was twenty years younger I'd give Alisha a run for her money over you". Julian walked over and gave her a hug "I knew you sounded good over the phone but you look like a model."
"Thanks Ma Carrie and I believe it would have been hard choosing between you two."
"Girl he has a silver tongue too, you have your hands full." Ma Carrie laughed.

We talked for a while before I got up leaving Julian behind so I could to talk to Tommy. "Hey Tommy do you think your parents would want to see me?"
"No they think you're the one that put me up to everything." I hugged Tommy
"I'm sorry."
"Why, because you gave me the courage to live instead of being ruled by them." Tommy sat on the sofa. "My family thinks I've turned on God because I won't do as I'm

told but God gives us free will and my instructions should come from God not man. Dad says I killed Senior with my evil ways by following you because you were conceived in evil. Alisha Senior knew I loved you and he encouraged me to marry you before and after Natasha."

I was shocked and couldn't hide it. "He did?"

"Yes he loved you and thought we would be the perfect couple. My father wanted me to be with Lisa so Senior stayed out of it." Senior died while Tommy was traveling so I didn't go to the funeral.

Tommy and I ended up in the kitchen preparing some food when everybody joined in, even Ms. Daniels. We sat around eating and talking until sleepiness set in and one by one everyone went to bed leaving me and Tommy to clean up. The next morning started as it had ended as Tommy and I prepared breakfast Julian came in with Millie followed by Ma Carrie and Ms. Daniels ending with Isabella. Ma Carrie blessed the food. "I am just so thankful to have my babies here with me at the same time with their family. It does my heart good so Tommy I can't wait until you and Isabella have that baby."

"What baby Ma Carrie?" he exclaimed.

"Boy don't play with me I know that child's pregnant and for a change it's real and more than likely yours."

"Isabella, are you pregnant?" Tommy asked in a slow steady tone.

"I'm not sure Thomas." She said as tears formed in her eyes because she was ashamed.

"Well I went out and bought a test this morning because I want a god child and Millie needs some cousins." I blurted out as I waved the box around in the air. Tommy snatched the test out of my hand and walked with Isabella to their bathroom. They came back down stairs "I know it's not done that fast" Julian said with excitement.

"No but we wanted to finish breakfast. Tommy said with a laugh and ran back upstairs. A few minutes later Tommy came in looking sad. "Tommy you're a daddy." I started screaming before he could answer.

"Alisha I was trying to do the fake sad bit but as usual you messed it up."

"Well you've never been good at that plus Ma Carrie said it yesterday and that was all the proof I needed."

"Why did you by the test?" Julian asked

"Because everybody can't rely on old folk wisdom."

"Who you calling old?" Ma Carrie said shaking her finger as we laughed. Tommy and Isabella kissed as we congratulated them. Tommy hushed the room "I have one more announcement we are moving closer to Alisha as soon as I get a job." Ma Carrie gave a nod of approval.

Everyone went their separate ways. Julian and I cleaned up the kitchen while Ma Carrie and Ms. Daniels took Millie for a walk in the nearby park. Ma Carrie and Ms. Daniels rested on a bench and talked as Millie played. Twenty minutes later they walked back because Millie and Ma Carrie needed a nap. Julian and I were sitting on the porch swing when they walked up. Millie climbed up in my lap and went to sleep. Julian picked her up. "Julian, what are you doing?"
"I'm taking her upstairs so she can be comfortable"
"But I want to hold her."
"You need some sleep to so why don't we all go upstairs and take a nap."
"Yes Daddy." I said slapping his butt
Tommy met us at the door with two sets of golf clubs "Tommy, what are you doing?" I asked.
"Julian and I are going to play golf."
"But Julian will only play with a special set of clubs."
"I know these are his clubs." Tommy said

handing the clubs to Julian.

"Julian you didn't bring your clubs." I said as I turned to look at him.

"Alisha since I met Thomas I've been playing golf with him so sometimes I would spend the weekend with him down here on the golf course. Forgive me for not telling you how close we were." Julian had a panicked look on his face.

"Julian I knew that but I didn't know it was this bad you've been cheating on me with golf." Tommy and I laughed because Julian thought I was upset. I kissed Julian "Go play after you put Millie in the bed."

I was awakened by Isabella walking into the room. "Alisha, are you awake?" she whispered

"Yes Isabella, how may I help you?"

"I want to help you Alisha." I thought here we go again with the stay away from Tommy speech. "Forgive me for my harsh words and my actions when I met you. I became insanely jealous about Thomas within the last few weeks. I don't know what came over me that night and dancing like that in front of your husband I am so embarrassed."

"It was the drink you had and all is forgiven so if I've offended you I ask that you forgive me."

"No you haven't you've been nice in spite of my actions' that tells me you really love Thomas and he is your friend."

"Let's start over. Hello I'm Alisha Tommy's best friend."

"Hello I'm Isabella Thomas's new best friend." We smiled and hugged because I realized as his wife she was his new best friend. We talked until Millie woke up "Bella" Millie said as she reached for her. "Would you like to go out and get something eat, my treat?"

"Yes that sounds great." I went down stair to check on Ms. Daniels and Ma Carrie but they were fast asleep on the sofa. The three of us went out to eat. When we got to the place I told Isabella the best dishes on the menu. After we placed our order I saw Tommy's mother and father. "Hello Mr. and Mrs. Ponder."

She replied, "Hello Alisha" as Mr. Ponder rolled his eyes. "I see you're here visiting Thomas," but before I could answer their food was ready and he rushed her out the door.

"They don't like me."

"It's not you, he's just mad because he can't control Tommy anymore."

"My parents were like that because I was to marry another man but I fell in love with Thomas."

"Love conquers all." We laugh as we picked up our order.

When we got back Ma Carrie and Ms. Daniels were sitting on the porch. "I picked you up you sleepy heads some lunch." "Thanks Lisha baby. I was wondering where everybody ran off to." Ma Carrie said "You know I have it made working for you Alisha. I get to rest on your vacation and you bring me food." Ms. Daniels chuckled. We sat on the porch and ate enjoying the beautiful day with laughter and hearty conversation.

A few hours later Tommy and Julian pulled up with his brother Marcus. They were laughing as they argued about who was the best and who cheated while playing golf. Tommy walked to the porch and greeted us. Isabella got up because she wanted to lay down and Tommy quickly followed. Ms. Daniels took Millie in the house to change her.

I yelled from the porch "Hello Marcus." "Hi Alisha." He smiled as he waved from the yard.
"How's your wife?" I yelled.
"She's great as a matter of fact she's on her way to pick me up." He said walking towards the porch.

"Do you have any kids yet?" I asked throwing him off because I knew he never wanted kids.

Ma Carrie chimed in. "No they won't give me any." She folded her arms and pouted as she got up and walked into the house.

"No we don't want any. I should've done like Thomas and got the heck out of here." He whispered looking around.

"Well it's never too late but you have to do what makes both of you happy." I smiled because I knew how he felt about the family and church traditions.

Marcus had a beautiful wife. They met in college and she wanted to move after she graduated with her master's in business. "It would make us happy to move and open our own Funeral Home in New Orleans." He said.

That's a big step and I will pray for you." I admitted rubbing his shoulder

Kashia pulled up. She parked and walked up to Marcus giving him a kiss as he went put his clubs in the car. "Hey Alisha I didn't know you were here." She said as she hugged me. "We just got here."

"Oh so how is Millie?"

"She's good." I said.

Kashia leaned over and whispered "Did you know about her?" She said motioning with her eyes.

"Yes." I chuckled. "Tommy came by my house before he came home." I leaned forward and whispered, "Why does everyone think we have more than just a friendship?"

"Have you ever seen the way he looks at you?"

"Girl please." We laugh and then she got serious on me. "Now I need the 411 on that tall hunk of a man who was with them. He use to come down here all the time with Thomas and then he went on that break so I need to get the info for a few women."

"His name is Julian, he's rich, retired and oh yeah the most important thing he's my husband." I said with a smile as she cried out in laughter while holding her stomach "You already have haters because of Thomas now they are going to despise you. Girl these women saw him today and did a phone tree trying to find out who he was." We laughed while Julian and Marcus looked at us from the yard and shook their heads. "His desperate sisters are on their way over here to meet him. Can I stay I have to see this cause I can't stand those hateful heifers."

The family didn't like her either.

We sat on the porch and talked while Marcus and Julian went in the house for a drink before returning to the yard to play with their clubs. Twenty minutes later we saw headlights when the car parked and Tommy's sisters were getting out of the car. They asked for help getting the food out of the car as the younger one, she was well built, flaunted for Julian but he ignored her causing her to try harder by blatantly flirting. We laughed on the porch as they brought in the food. "Hi Alisha I didn't know you were here." Brenda the older of the sisters said. The younger one Victoria was too busy following Julian. "Hi Victoria" I said.

"What are you doing here?" she said rolling her eyes.

"Tommy came to see me last week but had to leave the next day so we came out to see him."

"That was sweet, where is Millie?" she asked turning her attention to Julian

"She's in the house with the nanny." Julian said.

"Siddity bitch" she whispered as she walked into the house.

Kashia almost fell out of her chair laughing. She grabbed my arm and pulled me into the house.

Victoria was making a fuss over Julian when Ma Carrie walked in "Why are you throwing yourself at that man like a

desperate floozy sit your fast tail down."
She wave Ma Carrie away and made a
hunching motion with her shoulders as if
she didn't understand Ma Carrie's remark.
We walked into the kitchen. Julian was
nervous so he walked over and embraced
me as he whispered, "I didn't pay her any
attention or flirt back."
 Victoria turned up her nose, "Is that your
friend Alisha?"
"No I'm her husband." Julian said as he
kissed me "Oh and thanks for the food my
baby's eating for two so I know she's
happy." By this time Kashia was on her
knees laughing and Marcus had tears in
his eyes. Tommy walked in "What's going
on in here?"
Kashia told him through tears of laughter
"Your desperate sisters brought all this food
over her to impress Alisha husband, I mean
what they thought was a single man." That
caused Ma Carrie to laugh and Tommy
burst out laughing. Julian just held on
tight to me and whispered, "Baby I didn't
know." I smiled and shook my head.
Brenda stormed out but Victoria screamed
"Thomas is fucking you wife now." That
caused an avalanche of laugher. She
narrowed her eyes and yelled "He is in love
with your wife and..." She threw her hands
up and stormed out after she realized we

were not going to stop laughing at her. I
turned to Julian and said "Baby you can't
help it because you make women go crazy
but what you can help is your reactions to
their actions and don't you forget it." I
tapped him on the nose with my index
finger and spun around. "Is anyone
hungry?" I said pulling out plates and
serving spoons as we dug in.

Twenty minutes later Tommy's phone
rung. "Hello" he pointed and mouthed this
is my Dad. "Yes sir I understand." Tommy
hung up laughing, "You should be ashamed
of yourselves that was devastating to those
poor girls psyche." Tommy pulled Isabella
closer while rubbing her belly he said, "I
can't wait until me move and start our new
life because I refuse to be a controlling
father"
Marcus stood up "Man are you having a
baby?" Everyone knew how much Tommy
wanted children. "I'm going to be an Uncle.
Wait, does dad know and you said move?"
"We are moving closer to Alisha."
"Man I'm happy but I'm the last son and I
need to get out of here first."
"Well as soon as I get a job I'm gone sorry
Marcus."
Kashia walked over to Marcus and rubbed
his back "Baby we can always leave now

and move in with my aunt until we get on our feet."

"I just don't want to do that." Marcus said as he caressed her hand.

Tommy jumped up and pulled out his checkbook "What if I write you a check for ten thousand dollars and when you get the home up and running give me a share and we'll call it even."

Kashia's eyes lit up and she stared smiling but Marcus said "We can't do that."

Ma Carrie chimed in, "Why not you went to school and got the training so go for it because everybody needs a little startup money."

Julian gave his to cents, "Marcus I have some contacts there and we'll talk about getting a job and house for you guys."

"I know let's do this I need to marry Isabella and I'll pay you to do it if you marry us right now." Tommy started looking around and thought about what he said, "Forgive me for lying to everyone."

Ma Carrie looked up "You were lying to yourself I knew y'all weren't married. When are you children going to learn I'm old not stupid." Ma Carrie stood up, "I just want to say it wasn't old wisdom that made me realized Isabel was pregnant so am I really the only one that noticed her belly?"

I looked around but she had on a big shirt.

"No I never noticed."

Kashia said, "I thought she was just fat."

"Thomas you didn't notice she was getting bigger?" Julian asked.

"I thought it was from her changing appetite so I didn't want to say anything to hurt her feelings." Tommy looked at her "Isabella why didn't you tell me you were pregnant?"

"My mother found out and was going to tell my father so we had to leave."

"But why didn't you tell me?"

"I was afraid. My mother said once you found out you would leave me but then I saw how happy you were about Alisha and felt guilty."

"Baby I love you and I will never leave you." That night Tommy and Isabella were married by his brother and we flew out Sunday morning.

That Monday when I pulled into the driveway I saw Rafael, Mrs. Steinberg son, sitting on the porch. My heart sank because before I left Mrs. Steinberg had not been doing well. "Good morning"

"Hi Alisha its mom she passed last night."

"Are you alright?" I asked as I open the door "Would you like to come in to talk about it?"

"Yes just for a moment." He came in and

116

sat down and talked and cried for about thirty minutes before he gave me the funeral information we hugged and he left.

Julian made me stop bringing Millie to work with me after we hired Ms. Daniels so she could have a normal childhood. Twenty minutes later the door bell rung so I ran from the back to get it when I opened the door and Mikael was standing there. He grabbed me and started kissing me. I tried to stop him but I couldn't. "Mikael stop" I said through his kisses and tried to push him away. Mikael let me go. "Alisha you act like you're not happy to see me."
"Mikael I am but I can't kiss you like that I'm married."
"Me too Alisha, when I found out you were married it broke my selfish heart so I decided to reevaluate my life and revamp my priorities."
"So where is she?"
"I'm married to my life's purpose."
"I have an appointment in about five minutes so we will have to talk later." I said
"Then I will sit here until you're done." He said sitting down
"No come back and we can do lunch on you."
"I'll be back." He said walking out of the clinic.

I called Julian to ask if it was cool for me to go out with him but it went straight to voice mail and my appointment was there. "Hello Mr. Mumford come in and have a seat." He followed me back to my office. Our session lasted for an hour and I called Julian again but it went to voice mail again. I began to call his mother when my next appointment came so I had to hang up. My day was full and before I knew it Mikael was back and he brought our lunch. We talked and ate and talked and ate and talked until my next appointment arrived. Mikael kissed me on the forehead and said goodbye. I finished my last appointment by six and called Julian on my way home but it went to voice mail again. I said a prayer cut the radio on and lost myself in hope. Forty-five minutes later I pulled up next to Julian's car so I parked and ran inside. He was in the shower so I ran in with my clothes on. "Baby, what are you doing?" he said.

"I've been calling you all day and my calls have been going to voicemail." I said hugging him.

"It's good to be loved and appreciated but can I get out of the shower first." I hopped out, put on a robe, and went down stairs. Hello Ms. Daniels. Why is Millie sleep?"

"She said she's not feeling well."

"Now I really feel bad for working so long."
"Alisha please you have me and I will take care of her." Julian came down stairs and grabbed me. "There's my baby momma what's going on?"
"I tried to call you to let you know Mikael is in town and he came by for lunch."
"And you told him no so what's the problem?"
"I didn't tell him no and Mrs. Steinberg died last night."
"Let's go upstairs and talk excuse us Ms. Daniels." Julian snatched me by my arm causing me to stumble up the stairs. "What the fuck do you mean you didn't say no?"
"I had lunch with him and he kissed me when I opened the door."
"What else did you do."
"Eat and talked."
"You let him..."
"No Julian we ate food at my office."
"Is that all you almost made me lose it for no reason? Hell I kissed you when I tried to push up on you while you were with Alonzo." He paused and looked at me. "Did you go as far with him as you did with me?"
"No I kept my mouth closed and pushed him off."
"I'm good with that." Julian started kissing me "Baby give me that special treat." I put my hands behind my back squatted and

eased my tongue around his throbbing passion. I slid back and forth on his throbbing love until Julian grabbed my head as he dug his toes in the carpet and rammed his exploding passion into my awaiting mouth until he could go no further. With each moment of pleasure he thrust faster and faster until Julian gave up his essence and fell to his knees I followed him causing a vacuum until every drop was mine. "I need a shot of the sex juice Thomas brought before you kill me."
"Please you started it and take some tonight"
"I am because last night you made a brother weak." Julian and I had some type of sexual encounter every day and I loved it.

I kissed Julian and went down stairs to check on Millie she was eating dinner. "How are you feeling, Millie?"
"Mommy I ate candy."
"Ms. Daniels did she see Mr. Avery today?"
"Yes he was at the park."
"He gave her too many sweets." I said
"That reminds me he said Alonzo will be home soon."
"Thanks Ms. Daniels." I sat down next to Millie and Julian came down stairs. After we ate I got Millie ready for bed as Julian

cleaned the kitchen. We read her a bed time story together and she fell asleep.

I went to our bedroom and took a shower while Julian locked up the house. Suddenly I remembered the new shower gel I had just bought so I keep the shower running and jumped out to get. Julian was at the edge of the bed he had his back towards me and was going through my phone. Stepping back into the bathroom door I made some noise so he would know I was coming out. "Hey baby hand me that shower gel on the dresser." I startled Julian so he jumped up and drop my phone.
"What did you say Alisha?"
"The shower gel on the dresser, it's the pink and black bottle." Julian brought it to me and kissed me on the forehead before asking, "Alisha can I trust you?"
"Yes Julian why would you ask me that?"
"No reason I was just asking." I jumped back into the shower.

Julian's ex-wife realized she had messed up and wanted Julian back. They had lunch today and she told him some things about her and about me that caused him some concern. When I told him Mikael had dropped by unannounced for no reason it gave him a reason to question my actions.

When I got out of the shower I put on his favorite sexy piece of lingerie and walked into the bed room. Julian was sitting at the edge of the bed with his hands over his face. "Julian, is everything alright?"
When he looked up at me I could see he had been crying. "Alisha, would you cheat on me?"
"No I would never want to lose our family." I kneeled in front of him. "Why would you ask me that?"
"My children are not mine and they're not the man my wife was cheating on me with either so I don't know who she was with or if she really loved me." Julian pulled me closer as he looked into my eyes, "Alisha when you have the baby I need a DNA test."
"Julian I'll do whatever it takes to ease your mind."
Julian hugged me "Can I just hold you tonight?"
"Yes Julian." We kissed and got in bed. Julian rubbed my belly as he held me and I placed my hand on his leg. Within minutes I fell asleep but was awaken by Julian calling my name. "Alisha"
"Yes" I said as I groaned in the mist of my sleep.
"Baby I found out my children are not my children and the man that has been sleeping with my wife is not the father

either." I could hear the hurt and confusion in Julian's voice but I knew he just wanted to vent because he told me that earlier so I just listened and rubbed his leg to comfort him. "Now I wonder how many men she slept with and for how long?" Julian sat up in bed so I turned over and lay in his lap. "I never cheated on her with anybody but you and she was cheating on me the whole time." Julian let out a sigh. "The week before we got married he picked up the kids and she gave him the results of the DNA test." I could tell Julian was crying but I just squeezed his leg and kept quiet until he wanted me to talk. "I didn't even want to marry her but I couldn't have you so I settled and we had a wonderful life until the day she left me. I never knew she cheated with anyone except Carlton." Julian slid back down in the bed and I lay on his chest. "Who else was she fucking and how long did she fuck him?" Julian sat up "Alisha look at me." I sat up and looked at him. "Rasheda told me she saw you with another man last week at the Shay Lounge is that true?"

I wanted to say Julian we were together all last week but I knew he needed to be reassured. "No Julian that is not true."

"Are you sure because Mikael has been here for a week."

"Yes Julian and I didn't know he was here until today when he stopped by."

"Are you faithful to me Alisha?"

"Yes Julian." I was getting annoyed but I knew this was important to him

"Are you talking to any other men?"

"No Julian."

He got up and picked up my phone. "Why do you have four restricted calls on your phone and two unknown text?"

I opened the call log. "Julian only one of the restricted calls were answered and the text were not replied to."

"Why didn't you erase them then?" I knew then she was the one that placed those calls but this was not the time to try proving it. "I'm waiting Alisha."

"Julian I don't know."

"Is this the code you use to meet each other?"

"Julian look at the dates and time we were together on those days."

"You could've met him later that night."

"Julian we were having sex two of those day at the clinic because you couldn't wait, I went to lunch with Terrance's Ex's as usual on Friday and your mom on the 11th."

"Well you could have..."

"Julian stop it I refuse to let this woman put doubts in your head about our relationship."

"You said she worshiped the ground I walked on." He barked.

"Julian she did but that didn't mean she was perfect."

"Alisha, I would die if I found out you're not carrying my child."

"Well Julian you will live to see this through because this is your child."

"Are you still in love with Alonzo?"

"Why would you ask me that?" I knew I still loved him but I couldn't tell Julian that.

"Don't answer me with a question yes or no is what I need." I turned over to go back to sleep, "Alisha answer me."

"You are the one that was missing in action today. I called you several times but the phone went to voice mail and you never returned my calls." I sat up in bed. "I get home and you are taking a shower after you just left your ex-wife that told you your current wife was cheating on you. I'm going to sleep while you ponder your action today because I've never been MIA but you have been more than once in the past couple of days." I turned over and Julian walked out.

In the wee hours of the morning Julian was searching under the covers for my warm passion as he kissed and caressed me from my toes to the source of my warm passion I grabbed his head and swirled my hips until I exploded. Julian pushed inside of me slowly as he whispered in my ear, "Baby I'm sorry please forgi..." Before he could finish he convulsed and gave up his essence. Julian kissed me and between each kiss he asked for forgiveness. "Alisha I know I don't last long enough to satisfy you unless I drink Thomas's sex juice so I give it to you every day and that causes me to be insecure."

"Julian I've never complained about our sex life because I know you give me all you have"

"Alisha when I first met you I was quick with a condom and now I'm even quicker. I thought that over time I would get use to the feeling but it gets better and better every day." Julian sat up "The Aguardiente de Orujo works pretty good but I don't drink like to use it and sometimes I forget about."

"Julian the main thing is do I complain?" I asked as I climbed up behind him placing my chin on his shoulder.

"No you have never complained but I don't know if I can keep up."

"Don't worry about that, just keep being the man I fell in love with and we will be good." Julian turned around and kissed me.

That weekend we attended Mrs. Steinberg funeral and I had to be present for the reading of the Will. Mrs. Steinberg left Millie some money in a trust until she was eighteen and left me her property that was already becoming a Community Center. We had talked about doing that for a couple of years and she was working on all the red tape and political aspects. That was the perfect opportunity for me to retire and help others. She had already put everything in place for the new Center and within months after her death the two story Community Center would be a reality. She had them start the construction after she moved in with Rafael.

Husbands Secret

Julian and Tommy were still house hunting because they wanted to live near a golf course. Tommy found a job with a major company and they moved in with us until they could move into their own house. Isabella and I had become good friends. She was teaching me Spanish and was due any day. Ma Carrie came a few months later because she wanted to be there for the birth of Tommy's first child. I allowed other Therapists and Counselors to work with me in the evening so they could build relationships with the community and a clientele, which allowed me to work fewer hours and focus on the new Community Center.

Wednesday morning was the start of a beautiful day I was in my seventh month while Isabella was almost two weeks past her due date. Julian couldn't keep his hands off of me and had stopped drinking Tommy's sex juice every day.

Julian would nudge me every morning at the same time to have sex. We would have sex at least three times a day and it would last thirty minutes to an hour at night it was like the bigger I got the longer he lasted.

"Alisha, wake up." He whispered nudging me in the back

"I'm up Julian how do you want me." I said rolling over.

"Baby anyway you can get and be comfortable." He said as he rose to his knees so I could caress his love with my tongue like I did every morning but as usual he couldn't take much without losing control.

"Baby I am a blessed man to have a wife like you." He said as he slowly slid between my legs and caressed my burning passion with his tongue until I cried out his name. Julian jumped up quickly sitting in a chair and made me straddle him backwards but in less than five minutes he had quickly given up his essence so I kissed him and took a shower while he got back into bed.

"Julian that's messed up you wake me up every morning for a few minutes and then go back to sleep." I turned up my mouth and slapped him on the butt as I walked by.

"Baby you know I'm quick when you're on top and if you quit working like I asked you

could be in here with me." I shot him a bird
and laughed.

Julian had been trying to get me to stop
working for months but I love helping
people so I didn't see it as work. What I
didn't know is that Julian would leave out
behind me for his flying lessons. I got
dressed and went downstairs. Isabella was
already up and sitting at the table waiting
on me. "Are you okay?" I asked looking at
her sad demeanor.
"Yes but I couldn't sleep so I got up early."
She sighed
"Are you sure you want to go with me
today?" I asked while rubbing her back.
"This baby isn't coming out until they take
it out." She said sadly.
"Let's go." I said in a cheerful voice to
change the atmosphere.

Isabella and I headed to the office but
stopped for breakfast on the way. When we
got to the clinic she sat in the waiting room
and watched TV. I had some paper work to
get done so I sat in my office and dozed off
because sleep was a luxury around Julian.
I had a new patient George Oscuro and he
was dealing with an addiction to sex as well
as other things. This man was very
attractive and women threw themselves at
him. He wanted a stable relationship but

his drive was more than one woman could take. I knew how he felt all too well. He hit on me several times during our first meeting but I pretended I didn't notice. I heard the doorbell ring and looked at the time it was already ten o'clock. I went up front to meet him. "Hello Mr. Oscuro how are you?" I said as he followed me into the office. We talked, worked on some techniques, and set up a schedule for regular appointments. Our time went over because he had a few questions so by the time we finished Julian was there waiting for his lunch.

As I walked him to the door he recognized Julian. "Hey Julian man what are you doing here" George turned around towards me, "Is it okay to ask that?" "What you decide to talk about is up to you but I discourage any type of conversation outside of group in the office." I said with a reassuring smile but hiding my concern about his relationship with or even knowing my husband.
"Julian, are you coming tomorrow?" Julian turned pale as he tried to smile. He nervously turned towards me and said, "George this is my wife."
George looked surprised and said, "Man, I would've never thought you were married

nor had a baby on the way as wild as you are." I looked at Julian and anger burned inside me because I knew where George hung out and the things he liked to do for fun from our first meeting but George quickly extinguished those thoughts. "Dr. Carothers I know what you must think but Julian is in my flying class and he's a real daredevil."

"Oh really," I smiled as I turned towards Julian and if looks could kill he was dead "Thank you Mr. Oscuro I will see you next week." I said smiling as I opened the door. "Thanks, Dr. Carothers." We shook hands and he walked out.

"Baby I can explain." Julian quickly said but I turned and walked out of the room as Julian frantically followed me.

"Alisha baby," He said anxiously but I walked into my office and continued doing paperwork as if nothing had happened. "Alisha, so you're going to ignore me?" He demanded but I kept working as if I didn't even hear him. "Baby I'm sorry I lied to you." He said calmly before he gave up as he walked out full of regret he said "I'll see you at home tonight."

After I finished with my last appointment I walked them out and quickly walked into the bedroom to wake Isabella who appeared

to be missing. "Isabella, where are you?"
She was in the bathroom and couldn't hear
me calling her. I heard the toilet flush and
breathed a sigh of relief.

"I keep peeing on myself but when I go to
the bathroom nothing comes out but I keep
dripping." I knew that her water had broken
but I didn't want her to panic. "Let's lock-
up so we can go." While she cut off the
lights I called Tommy and told him to stay
calm and meet us at the hospital and he
called the doctor. I called Ma Carrie and
Julian to let them know about Isabella
while she was getting into the car. Isabella
and I left the clinic and headed for the
hospital.

"Alisha this isn't the way we usually go
home."

"No Isabella I need to make a pit stop."

"I'm not feeling too good and my back hurts
so I'm ready to go home to lie down." She
closed her eyes as I responded to her. "I will
get you in a bed soon so you can rest."
Within minutes I had pulled up in front of
the hospital and a nurse ran out with a
wheelchair. "Oh my god you drove yourself
to the hospital?"

"No I'm not the patient she's in the car."
Isabella contraction became stronger once
she got in the wheelchair." I parked the car
and went upstairs.

When I got upstairs a nurse looked at me and asked "Do you need a wheelchair?" as she got close to me she said "Is there anyone here to help you?"

"No I brought in Isabella Ponder and I was looking for her room."

"You're the pregnant woman that brought in a pregnant woman." She laughed

"Yes." I smiled because it was strange.

She said, "Follow me she's in room 612" I text the info to Tommy and Julian as we walked to the room. I walked into the room and Isabella looked up. "Where is Thomas?" as soon as she uttered the words he walked into the room. "Baby, how are you?"

"I'm in pain Thomas and I don't feel good." Tommy hugged Isabella and started looking around nervously. "Alisha this is real I'm about to be a father."

"I know Tommy and I am so happy for you." I sat down as he and Isabella continued their private conversation. When Ma Carrie and Julian walked in the doctor was right behind them. "Hello Mrs. Ponder are you ready to have the baby?" she turned around and looked at me "How far along are you?"

"I'm almost eight months."

"Please don't go into labor while I'm delivering this one because I only have two hands." We laughed "You don't have to worry I'm leaving." I walked over to Isabella and Tommy. "Call me when it's time for her to get ready to push. Love you guys and I'll be praying for you." I kissed Ma Carrie and walked out.

Julian ran behind me asking questions, "Alisha, are you still upset with me?"
"Julian we can talk later." I was tired and didn't have the strength for his need to have an adrenaline rush.
"Baby I want to talk now." Julian demanded as we entered the elevator.
I turned towards Julian "You lied to me about the pilot licenses and you don't love me enough to stop these stunts; therefore you just lost me?"
"Alisha you are being unrealistic about this situation." Julian grabbed my arm "Baby I am going to fly this weekend and that will be the last time I do it."
"Julian you don't have to explain yourself to me, do what you want you're grown." I walked to my car and drove home.

When I pulled up in the driveway Julian was right behind me. We walked in together. "Did she have the baby; how is she?" Ms. Daniels exclaimed
"No but she was at two centimeters when we left."
"I'm so excited."

"Me too" I said as I eased onto the sofa to play with Millie.

"Alisha, are you alright?"

"Yes I'm just tired and I miss my little angel"

Ms. Daniels put her hands on her hips "Girl I'm pulling rank kiss the baby and then get your butt up stairs so you can rest."

"Ms. Daniels I'll be okay." But the look on her face caused me to get my butt upstairs so I gave Millie a kiss and went to lie down.

Julian came upstairs about twenty minutes later because he was playing with Millie. "Alisha, are you sleep?" he asked as he walked over to the chaise lounge that I was resting on.

"No Julian." I answered with my eyes closed "Baby I didn't get my lunch today and now it's time for a snack"

"Let me take a shower first I feel icky." I uttered as I got up to take off my clothes.

"Baby I want you so bad." He said as he caressed my face and kissed my exposed shoulder.

I wasn't in the shower for two minutes when Julian got in and started kissing my back. I began to bathe a little faster because Julian was ready and he wasn't going to stop. I turned around and squatted in front of him so I could embrace his increasing passion and kept bathing. Julian pulled me up and gently rested my back on the shower wall and explored that which caused him to rise. Julian caressed the layers of my warm desire I placed my hands on top of his head and spread my legs wider so I could fill each stroke of his tongue causing my legs to wobble. Julian slowly slid his finger into my familiar passion and I moaned for more; his finger moved swiftly as his tongue moved skillfully in the mist of this pleasure. I pulled his head deeper into me as I continually swerved my hips harder until I erupted with passion and screamed his name like never before. My legs went limp so Julian carried me to the vanity end of the bathroom sink he pulled me to the edge and carefully placed the tip of his love in my essence eagerly as I begged for more of him with each plea he fulfilled my request giving more of himself until my warmth covered his love causing his movements to quickly increase with speed and depth as we moaned. I cried out in pleasure and became wetter as Julian grunted his feelings with each stroke. Ten minutes later Julian got so excited from the release of my essence causing the pleasure to become juicer he began to grunt and as they increased in volume. The force behind his thrust became stronger until he briefly rammed my head into the mirror releasing his essence with a thundering growl. Julian hadn't realized that my head had cracked the mirror and neither did I as he picked me up and carried me to the bed. Julian lay next to me and we kissed as if his passion was never released. Within minutes Julian was ready for me again. He motioned for me to mount him I hovered over him and bounced on the tip of his manhood causing his toes to curl and him to scream for more. I held his hands and bounced until the tip of his love left the warmth of my passion he eagerly craved more and squeezed me until he submerged himself deeper into the warmth of my love. Julian grabbed me by my hips as he rapidly bounced me up and down to his swift thrust he exploded in silent convulsions that cause him to abruptly rise up off the bed. "Damn baby can we fight more often?"

"That was on you." I said as I got up to get my phone.

"I know I was thinking I'm going to tear that ass up and remind her whose boss but shit I was the one screaming like a.... never mind." He sat up in the bed "Did Thomas call?"

"No not yet but I think I'm going to call and check on them.

"Baby do you think Ms. Daniels could hear

us?"

"You mean hear you screaming like a never mind?" I laughed as I walked into the bathroom.

"Very funny," he screamed as I closed the door.

After I finished I ran well wobbled out of the bathroom. "Julian, when did the mirror break?" Julian jumped up out of the bed and ran into the bathroom." Damn baby I think that your head did it come here." He said as he quickly walked over to check my head. "Does it hurt"

"No I'm fine but I do remember hitting my head."

"That proves two things you have a hard ass head like I've been saying and I was fucking the shit out of you or fucking your brains out." He stuck out his chest and said, "I give you permission to use either phrase," as he strutted out of the bathroom.

"You make me sick and remember I wasn't the one screaming like a never mind." I said as I unlocked my phone and called Tommy.

"Hey Alisha she's at eight centimeters and the doctors are going to give her something for the pain."

"Tommy well be down there in a few. Do you or Ma Carrie need anything?"

"No we're good but Ma Carrie is getting

tired."

"I'll take her home after the baby comes." I walked back into the bathroom to take a shower but Julian had beaten me to it.

"Julian, she's at eight centimeters." I said while he was in the shower.

"Good she should be ready to have the baby by the time we get there." I hopped in the shower after Julian.

When I walked down stairs Ms. Daniels whispered, "I told you to get some rest."

"I know but he's my husband."

"I understand you never deny your husband because it's to many women out there ready to pounce so you never send him out undernourished but your husband needs to understand you need rest." She laughed "Julian needs to understand you have to take care of...is she ready" I was confused by her question but when I saw Julian coming down stairs I knew why our conversation had to changed.

"Yes ma'am" I winked and said" She's eight centimeters" Millie ran over to me and gave me a hug and Ms. Daniels grabbed her.

"Mommy has to go see about Isabella, precious."

"Bella Bella." Millie screamed and wiggled out of Ms. Daniels arms so she could play.

Since Julian was driving I let my seat back and closed my eyes. "Baby are you still upset with me?"

"Yes Julian I am."

"But you had sex with me."

I rose up from the seat "I know"

"If you're upset with me why would you have sex with me?"

"Because you're my husband and like I told you when we got married nothing gets in the way of our sex life or our communication."

Julian had a puzzled look on his face. "But most women would've said no and you were tired too."

"Julian, I'm not most women and that's why some good men cheat."

"Alisha I would never cheat on you and I'm sorry for being so inconsiderate of you being tired."

"Like Papa said never is a long time and under the right circumstances anybody would or could do anything."

"Oh yeah I forgot you would know better than anyone Ms. Clean-up woman." Julian laughed

"You laugh now but I cleaned you and made you want to leave Rasheda."

"That was different."

"How was that different?"

"I had fallen in love with you the first night

I looked into your eyes."

"But I was the only woman you cheated on her with because I let you chase me then I had you wrapped around my finger after I released my fierce skills on you."

"Alisha really I had you hooked."

"Julian you couldn't last five minutes with me at first so when or how did you have me."

"This tongue had you whipped the first time I laid down my skills."

"More proof that I had you because when I met you tasting a woman was something you had only tried with me." I thought this man laid it down his first time but I couldn't tell him that because he was right. "I lied you were the first but you just had something a man wanted to taste." We pulled into the parking garage. "Alisha it was something about you that made me want to try something new and that thang tasted so good I couldn't stop." We continued to talk as we drove to the hospital.

Julian parked and helped me out of the car as we walked to the elevator I thought about what he said. As soon as we walked into the room we heard a baby cry and the doctor announce, "it's a boy". Tommy decided to name him Thomas Coleman

Ponder. If it had been a girl Isabella would've named the baby. Ma Carrie was at the warming table watching the nurses clean him up while Isabella fell asleep. Tommy stood next to her as the proud papa with tears in his eyes. Because Isabella was asleep Tommy gave the baby to Ma Carrie to hold. Tears ran down her face as she cooed with the baby. Ma Carrie looked up, "I never thought I would see this day nor did I think it would turn out like this but God knows what's best." Tommy and I looked at each other and smiled because we knew what she meant. We headed out thirty minutes later because Tommy took so long to eat the plate Ms. Daniels prepared for him.

Isabella and Lil Thomas or Cole came home on Friday and found out that the house they wanted would be ready for them to move into within two weeks. They had closed on the house with an agreement that the owners wouldn't be out for a month but it would be ready sooner so Tommy and his new family could move in sooner. We had already closed on our house two doors down but Julian want to remodel it before we moved in. Millie was excited about her cousin and couldn't wait to hold the baby.

I awake that Saturday morning feeling kind of strange in the pit of my stomach. "Julian." I called out and I sat up when he didn't answer. "Baby, where are you?" I called out. It was nine o'clock and he hadn't tried to get any so I was a little worried. I got up and looked in the bathroom but he was not there. I thought about Tommy and it dawned on me that they may have gone to play golf. Millie ran into my room. "Mommy Mommy" she screamed as she pulled my arm. "Millie let me get dressed and I'll fix breakfast." I turned around when I thought about her being in my room. "How did you get out of your bed?" I looked up and Tommy was standing in my room. "Alisha I took her out because you were still sleep and I didn't want to wake you." "Tommy what are you doing here?" Tommy had a puzzled look on his face. "I thought you were with Julian playing golf." "No Julian left out about an hour ago talking about his first and last time before the baby comes." "What?" I screamed as I whirled around. "Alisha I couldn't understand what he was talking about I was making a bottle for the baby and he started mumbling something." I smiled until I realized what Tommy was telling me I held my stomach as fear and panic over came me "He's going to fly anyway." I quickly grabbed my phone and called him but it went directly to voice mail so I left a message. I frantically searched for his mother's number in my phone. I dialed it but she didn't answer so I started praying because I woke up with an eerie feeling so I was scare that Julian might get hurt. My phone rung but my hands were shaking so profusely I could barely answer it. Tommy rubbed my back to calm my nerves and whispered, "Everything is fine, allow God to work it out." I hugged him before he walked out of the room with Millie.

My phone rang; it was Julian's mom returning my call. "Hi Mrs. Carothers this is..."
"I know who you are Alisha and its mom, is everything alright?"
"Have you heard from Julian?" I asked
"No honey why what happened?" she replied in an uncertain but calm voice.
"I think he went for his first flying lesson today."
"No he didn't Alisha because he dropped out weeks ago." She said with a sigh of relief.
"He didn't quit but lied to me and I found out Wednesday he was flying today." I said full of panic and fear. I tried to calm down because I remembered what Tommy said

after I prayed but it was not working. I could hear Donna in the background calling her husband. She came back to the phone "Alisha let me talk to Mike and find out what is going on." I could only make out parts of their conversation but it ended with "Leave the damn boy alone and let him fly." Donna came back to the phone. "Alisha he wouldn't tell me anything but I'll call you if I hear from him."

She hung up and I calmed down and join everyone down stairs. "Good morning family." I announced as I floated into the kitchen. "Mommy, sit down next to me." Millie cried as she pointed to the empty chair next to her. "Okay baby." I said as I kissed her forehead. Tommy sat a plate in front of me. "Did you find out anything?" "No and I'm not going to concern myself with it anymore." I smiled and nodded at Tommy so he would let it go and began to eat.

While we were eating my phone buzzed the text was from Alonzo he wanted to video chat with Millie so I replied asking for five minutes. "Millie daddy wants to talk to you."

Tommy turned around, "Tell Alonzo I said hello."

"Alright." I picked Millie up and we went to my office. I pulled up the screen, "Alonzo, are you there?"

"Yes Alisha where's Millie?"

She jumped up screaming "Daddy Daddy"
and I moved out of the way.

"Alisha are you pregnant?" he shouted

"Yes and Tommy said hello"

Alonzo text me, "Can we talk after I finish
with Millie." I replied that we could and he
talked with her for ten minutes as usual
because her attention span was not long
and she was bored. "Hold on Alonzo let me
get someone to watch her." Ms. Daniels was
on her way to change Millie already.

"Thanks Ms. Daniels."

"Alonzo I'm back and please let's talk not
argue." I said as I sat in the chair

"Alisha, when did you start seeing
Thomas?"

"What are you talking about?" I said with a
puzzled look.

"The baby I didn't know you were seeing
Thomas, did you get married?"

"No Alonzo I'm not pregnant by Tommy but
he got married and his wife just had the
baby Wednesday. They moved in with me
until they could move into their new
house."

"So who are you pregnant by?"

"My husband I got married a few months
ago." I could see the hurt in his eyes and I
wish I would've stayed out of his sight. "Do

I know him?" he sounded broken

"No Alonzo you don't," I didn't realized how much this would hurt him because he was with Ginger so I didn't tell him it was Julian.

"How long have you been married and when is the baby due Alisha?"

"About nine months and I'm almost eight months pregnant." I said in an uneasy tone.

"Well I'll be home in three months and you can introduce me to your husband."

"Alonzo I'm sorry if I hurt you."

"I doesn't matter anymore I lost you because of a foolish game and this hurt is mine to carry alone but I did start dating Ginger." I could tell he was not happy with her. "Well Alisha congratulations, good bye." Before I could say good bye he had logged off. I walked into the family room where Ma Carrie and Ms. Daniels were watching TV but their program had been interrupted by a special report. "Hey what are y'all watching it's not time for the news."

"Somebody has crashed a plane into the woods or a house or something."

I was still thinking about how hurt Alonzo was when it hit me that the TV said school. I quickly walked back into the family room. "What did they say?"

"A student pilot crashed into a house when

he lost control of the plane."
"Did they give a name?"
"No I don't believe so."
By this time I was crying and unknowingly raised my voice "Did they say if he was black, white, married, or anything?"
Ma Carrie looked at me and waved me over "Alisha you are going to make yourself sick, what's wrong?" she asked while Ms. Daniels tried to comfort me.
Between muffled words, heavy breathing and sniffing I said, "Julian was flying today for the first time." I fell to the floor and cried. My phone rang and Ms. Daniels ran to get Tommy. I picked up the phone and looked at the caller id it was Mike, Julian's father. Tommy quickly snatched the phone out of my hand and answered it. "Hello"
"My I speak with Alisha" you could tell he was crying.
"She just saw the news is it Julian?" Tommy said as he walked out the room.
"They believe it is but the bodies are so badly burned that identification is hard."
"What have they told you so far?"
"They are checking the dental records because several people are missing. The plane crashed into the hanger." Tommy could barely make out what he was saying because of the crying. "Tell Alisha I'm sorry for encouraging him to fly." He hung up

and Tommy walked into the family room. Isabella had taken Millie into their room to protect her from seeing me cry. I walked over to Tommy "What did he say?" "They don't know for sure because the bodies were badly burned but they are getting the dental records to match the bodies." I nodded my head while Tommy was talking and looked around the room. "Will you keep an eye on Millie I need to be alone to pray and think?" I pulled my phone out of Tommy's hand and walked upstairs. "She doesn't need to be alone in her condition." Ms. Daniels exclaimed. "She's strong and needs to be alone." Ma Carrie said as she sat on the sofa and begun to pray. Tommy joined her Ms. Daniels followed and Isabella came out to join in.

In my room I talked to God and let be known all of my fears and concerns. I paced back and forth praying until I got tired then I called Julian's phone so I could hear his voice again before I sat down and listen for Gods instructions. I sat there for thirty minutes and wrote down everything that came into my mind and then I picked up my bible and read until I fell asleep. I awake when Tommy walked into the room. "Ma Carrie said you need to eat to keep your strength up."

I looked at him and smiled "You look like you're scared."

"I am those ladies threaten me to come up here so you know who I am more afraid of." He laughed. "Are you okay Alisha?"

"Yes Tommy I know I need to eat for the baby that's why I calmed down is Millie alright?"

"She's good she didn't see anything."

Tommy put his arms around me and kissed me on the forehead and tears flowed down my face. "He didn't even speak to me today he just let me sleep." I hugged Tommy and cried until my phone went off.

Tommy answered it. "Hello"

"This is Julian's father Mike, is Alisha and the baby alright?"

"Yes they are doing well." Tommy talked without any facial expression to keep me calm but it annoyed me when he did that.

"I'm sorry for not calling sooner but his mother had to be sedated." You could hear the confusion and uncertainty in his voice.

"I understand just keep us up to date about everything."

"They did find his car but have yet to identify his body. Tell her to forgive me but he used me as his next of kin so he could keep his secret and now I'm glad he did."

"Thank you and I'll tell her." Tommy hung

up the phone

"What did he say." I asked as I anxiously awaited an answer.

Tommy talked slow and deliberately. "They found his car but have yet to identify his body."

"It's possible that he's alive and decided to leave with someone else." Tommy didn't want to upset me so he let me comfort myself with off the wall notions. "I'm going back down stairs to check on the little ones, don't worry well take care of Millie." I sat on the chaise lounge and started writing in between prayers, my past, and my life with Julian. I had fallen asleep and was awaken by the running shower. I got up to check and it was Julian so I undressed and joined him in what I realized was my dream. Julian roughly kissed me as I returned the pleasure until I tasted the stale liquor in his kisses and thought Lord please let my last moments with him be perfect. Julian was kissing me as if he was hungry and the kisses increased his hunger. Julian put me on the vanity and caressed my wetness with his absorbing tongue as I spread my legs wider until I gave his amazing tongue what it was searching for. Julian plunged his massive love into the pool of essence he created as he intensely immersed in the never ending juices awaiting for him. I gave my essence up over and over until our satisfaction mixed with the last thrust of pleasure. Julian fell to his knees "I love you Alisha and being your husband is all I need to prove who or what I am. As I struggle to get down from the vanity I ushered Julian to the bed and wrapped his arms around me quickly melting away in my never ending dream.

The next morning Tommy walked into my bedroom and walked out suddenly causing the door to slam. "Alisha" he yelled from the other side of the door.
I sat up in bed "What Tommy." I said still trying to recall the dream.
"Are you alright?"
"Thomas shut the fuck up with all that yelling man we're trying to sleep."
Tommy slowly opened the door. "Julian is that you?"
He sat up in the bed "Thomas who else would be in the bed with my wife." Tommy started yelling, "He's here he's here."
"Man shut up I have a head ache damn."
I started hyperventilating "Alisha." Julian shook me after wrapping a sheet around him. "Thomas shut up and help me man." I passed out and fell back onto the bed. Ms. Daniels ran into the room "What's wrong Thomas?"

"Alisha passed out and Julian is in the bed."

Ms. Daniels started praising God.

"My pregnant wife has fainted, Ms. Daniels has starting talking in another langue and Thomas you look like you've seen a ghost; what in the hell is going on?"

"Julian you're dead."

"What the fuck I'm right here."

"The school you went to was destroyed when the plane crashed."

"The plane crashed?" Julian sat down in disbelief and the room suddenly calmed down. "Thomas what happen?"

"The flight school was destroyed when a student pilot crashed into it killing several people. They were burned beyond recognition." Ms. Daniels had gone down stairs to share the news with Ma Carrie. I sat up grimacing. "Baby I'm sorry I put you through all of that." Julian said as he hugged me. "Call your parents." I said quickly handing him my phone after I dialed the number.

"Hey dad it me Julian, where's mom?" Julian looked at the phone "Hello, hello is anyone there?"

"Just stay on the phone." I said pushing it to his ear.

"Julian is that really you?" His father said slowly

154

"Yes Dad it's me" Julian uttered as tears rose up in his eyes.

"I thought you were dead." He humbly voiced before he quickly pulled himself together. "Say hello to your mother."

"Mother it's me Julian." Julian had a downcast face and looked as if he was fighting back tears so I leaned over to embrace him.

"Is it really you?" she gasped

"Yes Mother." Julian muttered as tears fell.

"I won't believe it until I put my hands on you." She said frantically.

"I'm getting dressed to come over." Julian said wiping his face as he stood up.

"I love you Julian." She sincerely uttered.

"I love you too mama." I kissed his moist cheeks as tears rolled down his face.

"Come on Alisha let's go to my parents' house." We got dressed and headed out the door.

During our ride Julian opened up. "Alisha I am so sorry for doing this behind your back but I wanted to do one last thing before I became a father." Julian held my hand. "Alisha I felt like I'm not enough for you so I had to accomplish something great to impress you but that morning I heard you cry out don't die Julian so when I got to the school I was nervous. George felt uncomfortable with it too so we went to his house and talked while we drank and I passed out. When I woke up they were playing cards so I played a few hands drank a little and he was too drunk to drive so one of his girls brought me home." I slowly pulled my hand away from his. "Alisha I didn't touch any of those women and I would've called but I was having fun and time just slipped away."

"Julian if you need to have fun let me know because I will divorce you; allowing you that freedom and as far as you wanting to accomplish something for me try not being selfish for a change, everything you've done so far is to prove your manhood. That has been your own pleasure not something that would please me. Julian you are a wonderful man and perfect husband and father so just be who you are and let me love that not this daredevil stunt man."

"Alisha I promise no more stunts." We talked until we drove up to the mansion and the butler parked the car. Julian quickly ran up the stairs as I quickly wobbled behind him. He turned around to help me but I waved him off, "Go see about your mom." Julian disappeared up the main staircase but I knew where he was going. When I walked into the room his ex-wife was hugging him as his stepchildren

delighted in his presence. "Hello mom and
Mr. Carothers." I said breathless.

Donna yelled out "Alisha, bring that belly
over here." As I walked past his ex-wife she
rolled her eyes and whispered to Julian.

"Hello mom, how are you feeling?"

"Better now that my son is home." She felt
my belly "Where's the baby?"

"He's in there."

"It's a boy?"

"No" Julian said as he walked over. "We are
having a girl and she'll be just as beautiful
as her mother." He said as he kissed my
nose.

"You look familiar to me." His ex-wife said.

I smiled and said, "Oh really"

"Yes aren't you Julian's cousin that would
accompany us on vacations and family
trips?" She put her hands on her hips and
with a smirk she said, "Talk about kissing
cousins."

"I'm not his cousin."

"I know payback is hell isn't that right
Julian darling?" she winked at him as if
they shared a secret.

Donna didn't care for Rasheda anymore but
because of the grandkids she tolerated her.

"Julian where were you yesterday?" His
mother asked.

"With me" Rasheda jumped in to say "He
called and came over before the kids got up

and we reminisced about old times." She
smiled at me after she finished talking.
"Mr. Carothers can I get a chair because I
can't keep standing up in all this bull...
Thanks Julian" I smiled as he brought me a
chair and assisted me when I sat down.
"You need to call me dad because you're
family." Mike never liked Rasheda so she
called him Mr. Carothers. "Keep going
Julian." He said turning his nose up at
Rasheda.
"I was at a classmate's house. I didn't want
Alisha to know she had won because then
she would know how much control she had
over me." Julian smiled at me as he
squeezed my hand. "I left my phone at
home and I was drinking so much that I
passed out. Later that night I got a ride
home and found out what happened this
morning"
Rasheda chimed in again, "sounds like one
of the story's you would tell me when you
were with your cousin or Melissa." Julian
became enraged and mouthed something to
Rasheda and she gave an evil smile in
return.
"Rasheda I need you to leave" Mike said
and everybody's mouth dropped.
"If I leave I'll never bring the kids back."
"I don't care they aint my blood no way and
the only one you'll be hurting is them but

we know what kind of selfish low life you are."

"Mike, don't talk to her like that." Donna exclaimed

"Why not she is giving Alisha the blues and Alisha is the one carrying our grandchild."

"That is not Julian's baby you will see after that blood test I told him to get. She is not as sweet as you think she is." Rasheda turned her angry stare towards me. "Ask him about Melissa, yeah your man has secrets but I always knew when you were with her." Rasheda said as she turned her furry towards Julian.

"But she is sweeter than you, now leave." Mr. Carothers belted.

Rasheda grabbed her stuff "You will pay for this and oh yeah Julian Melissa is showing." she said as she stormed out laughing. I notice Julian wiped something from his face.

"Mike why did you do that, I may never see my grandkids again."

"That's what court orders and judges are for."

"But were not their biological grandparents."

"They don't know that and I was tired of her being here so I talked to a lawyer."

"What if they rule against us, I may never see them again?" She replied nervously

"The lawyer said our case looks good so she will be served Monday." Mike folded his arms letting them know he was done with the matter. "Julian you have a beautiful wife and a child on the way all of that selfish it's about me crap is over." His father said standing to his feet. "I agreed with you until I saw the pain in your mother's eyes and I thought I had lost you." Mike placed his hand on Julian's shoulder. "Son I love you and I don't want to lose you like that." Julian and his father hugged as tears of joy ran down his mother's face. Mike was a no nonsense man and showed very little affection especially towards men so for him to hug his son was major. We talked for a while, ate lunch and said our good byes a few hours later. As we got in the car and drove home Julian said, "Baby I'm not cheating on you."

I answered him with my eyes closed "I know Julian I know." He held my hand as we drove home. I prayed that Melissa was not back in his life. She was a six month fling before he gave up everything for Rasheda why would she be back now. I raised my head and looked at my husband. I could see the evidence of her all over him but why now and how did I miss that secret lust.

When we got home the three of us spent the rest of the day together.

Neighbor's

Tommy had only twenty-four hours left to put the finishing touches on their new home; which took an extra four weeks to get done. His family and friends we coming to his house warming party. The church charted a bus for the six hour ride and it was packed. Marcus and Kashia came in the day before. She helped me with last minute decorating ideas Isabella had while Marcus, Tommy, and Julian played golf. The party planning was done by "Dream Big Events" one of Julian's cousins. We realized Tommy's finishing touches was getting in as much golf as he could before the guest arrived. We decided to stroll down the street to my new house while the guys played golf after we finished. Millie and Lil Thomas were at home with Ms. Daniels and Ma Carrie.

We walked out of the house at five o'clock and were turning into the driveway when the guys drove up. "Where are you going?" Julian asked from the rear passenger window.

"I wanted to show the girls the house."

"You can't."

With puppy dog eyes I asked, "Why not?"

"That's not going to work" he said as he got out of the car. I pouted and stomped my foot. "So now you want to throw a tantrum." Julian embraced me and kissed the top of my head. "I have a surprise for you and I don't want you to see it yet." I smiled and spun around to face Julian as everyone left. "What is it?"

"You're worse than Millie." He said with a robust laugh.

"Julian you know I hate surprises." I said as I pouted and wobbled behind him to catch up.

"Yes I do." He said as he laughed as he ran a few steps so I couldn't hit him.

When we got back to home we decided to eat out. The six of us piled up in Julian's SUV. As we drove to the restaurant we chatted about the party and life. Julian's phone kept going off with text messages so I picked up it up. "No Alisha put it down." Julian said while snatching the phone out of my hand. The passengers in the SUV looked at each other nervously. "Julian since when has it been an issue for me to look at your phone?"

"Alisha, Rasheda keeps sending me graphic text messages since the scare and I didn't want to upset you." He said as he gauged my reaction with glances. I knew he was not telling the truth but we had company so I said, "When is she going to stop harassing us?"

"Baby I don't know but I'll talk to the lawyer Monday morning." He said with a sigh of relief.

"Thanks for protecting my feelings baby." I said as I sat back in my seat. Even though I was extremely upset I had to keep my cool. Julian was cheating on me I thought to myself as we drove. After we got to the restaurant Julian called Richard and he came out to greet us. "Isn't this a nice place Marcus?" Kashia said "Yes it is baby." He leaned over and whispered in her, "I hope we can afford it."

Richard walked up to the hostess and said, "Give them whatever they want it's on me but Julian you have to leave a nice tip." He said as he patted Julian on the back and extended his hand as if the restaurant was on display. "Thanks Uncle Richard." Julian replied as he hugged him. We were escorted to our table. "Hello I'm your server tonight how may I help you." She said with a smile

"Monica is that you?" Julian said as he rose from his chair to give her a hug. He turned around and introduced her to us. "Everyone this is my sister in-law because I divorced Rasheda but not the family." We responded with a hello. "Monica this is my wife Alisha." I smile and nodded as did she. Julian sat down as she took our order. After she walked away we started talking. I leaned over and said to Julian, "She does look like a younger version of Rasheda." Julian nodded and kissed me on the neck as he whispered. "Let's go in the back so I can get some I'm hard as a rock." I eagerly smiled and looked around as he continued. "I haven't had my lunch and my breakfast was cut short because of Thomas."
"Where?" I said through a grin.
"Oh hell no y'all are not going anywhere just wait until you get home." Tommy said abruptly.
Julian looked at Tommy. "What are you talking about?" Julian said with a fake puzzled look but the grin on his face gave it away.
"You know what I'm talking about and its embarrassing just wait until you get home like normal people." Tommy said as he lower his voice.
"Thomas we are going to look at the view." Julian said as he stood up and grabbed my

hand.

"There is no view and you make too much noise, now sit down." Tommy stood up and pointed to the seat. Julian sat down and flagged down Monica "Make that a double." He said folding his arms and pouting. "Looks like the shoe is on the other foot." I turned to Julian and squeezed his pouting face and joking said, "Don't be mad cutie." We laughed as Marcus leaned over and whispered in his wife's ear causing her facial expression to change in to an agreeable head nod with a sly smile.

The appetizers came out with the drinks as we continued to laughed and talk. Julian finally gave in after he returned from the restroom. By the time the food came out we were fully engulfed in laughter and conversation. When we were leaving Julian gave Monica a four hundred dollar tip and told her to say hi to the kids and her husband. He gave her a hug and rushed towards me as I headed towards the exit. "Baby will you get the car I need to make a phone call" Julian said as he was pulling out his phone.

"I will." I walked over to catch up with the group and gave the valet our ticket.

Tommy looked around "Where's Julian?" "He had to make a phone call." I said distracted by my thoughts and Julian's strange behavior. Tommy pulled me to the side and whispered, "Is he upset because of what I said?"

"No Tommy it's not you." I said with a smile but the look in my eyes gave Tommy concern.

"Alisha he's not cheating on you is he?" Tommy said with a concerned look.

"I don't know?" I looked a Tommy with a hateful glance because I realized what was wrong with my husband. Julian walked out and asked, "Thomas would you drive us home I think I had one drink too many." This was strange to me because Julian nursed that one drink at dinner but his appearance had changed after the phone call. Tommy and I looked at each other and hunched our shoulders. The valet pulled up in the car and we piled in. Julian and I sat in the rear per his request.

On the way home Julian was obnoxious so I was glad when we turned onto our street. When we got there everyone said their goodbye's as we got out. I walked into the house. Tommy jumped out and pulled Julian aside before he walked in.

"Man, what's going on with you?" Tommy said.

"What, Thomas I can't have sex with my

wife when and where I want to?" Julian
said as he threw his arms in the air.
"No that's not what I'm talking about it's
the drinking and your strange behavior."
Tommy leaned on the railing. "Julian you
drink everyday now but when I met you it
was only on rare occasions."
"Thomas, do you know what it's like to be
with a woman like Alisha?" Julian said
sitting down as he wiped his face.
"What is she like?" Tommy was perplexed
because he thought I was the perfect wife.
"I crave this woman all the time but I can't
satisfy her." He yelled behind clenched
teeth. He leaned towards Tommy and said,
"What if she leaves me when Alonzo comes
back?"
"Alisha loves you and only wants to be with
you." Tommy sat down and looked Julian
eye to eye. "But if you don't straighten up
she's going to leave you not because of
another man but because of you."
"Thomas I love that woman and I will do
anything to satisfy her." Julian said
pointing at the house.
"That's good Julian but I think trusting her
is more important than what you're doing
right now." Tommy walked back to the car
while Julian sat on the porch.

Twenty minutes later Julian walked into oor room and ripped off my clothes and flipped me over caressing what he wanted. Julian viciously thrust himself in his choice of pleasure. I wanted to stop him but he was acting like an enraged animal seeking to satisfy a long awaiting passion. Julian grunted in a sick pleasure after fifteen minutes and rolled over on the bed panting heavily so I got up and cleaned myself up. When I came out of the bathroom Julian was whispering into the phone so when I got into bed I startled him. "Hey baby what are you doing?" Julian asked as he rolled over towards me. "Going to sleep" I said with closed eyes.

"Can I get some more?" he said as he eased up next to me.

"I can give you head, the back door or let you eat it but the coochie is ripped up and out of commission for penetration."

"Let me kiss it." Julian said as he helped me over to the chair and gently caressed my tenderness with his tongue. He squeezed my thighs and moaned as if I was pleasing him causeing my juices to flow and passion to quickly rise. I called out his name and freely released my essence for him to enjoy. Julian stood up and helped me get back in to the bed. Julian slid in behind me as he eagerly slid himself into a place causing voiceless screams of pleasure from both of us. Within minutes Julian gave a victorious cry as he released his essence. I fell asleep in his embrace.

That morning I felt Julian get up and go into the bathroom but he locked the door so I knew something was going on. When he came out he was dressed and said, "Alisha I'm headed out to play golf with Thomas so I'll see you later at his house." After I heard the car pull off I wobbled into the bathroom and started searching for what I didn't know for sure. I thought did I want to know Lord let him be cheating but not with her. I climbed up on the highest shelf and I saw my worst fear, Melissa was back. It took me less than an hour to find it but I did and put the evidence back before I got ready for the house warming party.

When I got down stairs our ride was already there. Ma Carrie looked at me with great concern. "Child what's got you in such a strange mood?" Ma Carrie put her hand on my stomach. "You sad and scared about that husband of yours don't be he's a good man y'all a work it out."
I smiled "Ma Carried I'm fine just tired from carrying this baby."
"You probably having that baby today something strange is going on with you." As

Ma Carrie and I walked to the car I could hear her praying. Kashia was driving and I was relieved. The men were already over there, Isabella; Kashia had taken her over there earlier. The car buzzed with chatter but I lay back with my eyes closed. Millie called out my name a few times but Ms. Daniels hushed her because she saw what Ma Carrie saw in me a deep sadness and lost.

When we got there the catering company had the food laid out and the flow was good. About thirty minutes later the bus pulled up and people started getting off and headed towards the house. Tommy's father pulled his son's over and talked to them. He let Tommy know he was proud of him while his mother held her first and only grandchild like he was gold. Everyone was talking, laughing, eating, and having fun. After an hour or so I got tired and went into the house to find a quiet room.

Julian found me sitting in a room by myself. "Hey baby, are you alright?" He said as he walked over. He was concerned because he could see that strange look as well.
"Yes Julian" I said with a solemn face.
"Alisha, are you in pain." He got on his knees next to me.

171

Tears rolled down my face "Julian I know."
"Know what Alisha?"
"That Melissa is back."
Julian fell to the floor as if someone had just knocked him over. "No she's not."
"Top shelf behind the black and silver plate I found the evidence this morning." I said as I stood up
"Alisha I can explain." He rose to his knees.
"No you can't but until we leave this party we are a happy couple." I walked out the door and Julian quickly followed in fear.

I found Tommy outside "Hey we are about to leave I'm getting tired so Julian is going to take me home" I said hugging him.
"I would ask you to stay but I can see something in your..."
I abruptly interrupted him "Tommy enjoy your party and call me later."
"Thomas this was nice and I am happy for you man." Julian said as he shook Tommy's hand so Tommy pulled him closer and whispered, "What is going on?"
"I can't tell you but come over later I might need your help, I think it's over." Julian walked off and Tommy watched as we pulled off.

On the way home Julian broke the silence. "Alisha, please don't leave me."
"How long have you been dealing with

Melissa, Julian?" I asked looking straight ahead.

"Alisha, please forgive me I can drop her and never look back." He said pleading

"How long Julian?" I asked as if I didn't hear him.

"Alisha you mean the world to me." Julian pulled over because he was distracted.

I squinted my eyes and yelled, "How fucking long Julian?" He was shocked because not only did I profanity I yelled at him. "Alisha." He pleaded.

I quit asking the question because I was getting angrier buy the second with his excuses. Julian looked around as if he was confused and he pulled off the road.

Tears rolled down my face but I never looked at him. I slowly turned towards him and asked calmly, "How long have you been snorting cocaine Julian?"

He held his head down in shame and responded, "I started a few weeks ago." He put the car in gear and started driving as we sat in silence. I closed my eyes and allowed the tears to roll down my face releasing the hurt and betrayal with each drop because I knew he was lying.

Full of confidence Julian said, "It was for you Alisha." I looked at him with pure hatred as my nostrils flared and evil thoughts went through my mind. I took a deep breath and turned my attention to the road before closing my eyes again. "Alisha I had more stamina and could keep it up longer." He exclaimed.

I thought as I sat up and glared at him does this muthafuka think I'm stupid. I folded my arms and grimaced in the pain that I could no longer hide.

"Alisha, are you alright?" he said placing his hand on my stomach when another contraction hit. I gripped the car door so I he wouldn't notice my pain. "Alisha, I felt your stomach tighten are you in labor?" Before I could say a word he quickly pulled over and called Tommy. "Thomas, Alisha is in labor I'm headed to the hospital and I'll call you when she's checked in." Julian hung up before he could respond. "Alisha I can't believe you are so stubborn." He turned to look at me when we approached a light. "What were you planning to have this baby without me after I dropped you off at home?"

Through clinched teeth and a contraction I told Julian "Shut the fuck up talking to me you low down muth...." I held my breath and held my head down while squeezing the door handle. When the pain stopped I lay back in my seat but Julian's head was like a bobble doll looking between me and the road with his mouth wide open.

When we pulled up to the hospital I looked back at Julian and said "I want a divorce" and hopped out of the car. I headed towards the elevators up to labor and delivery. Julian got there as they were taking me to my room. As they prepped me Julian quickly called Tommy, "Alisha asked for a divorce so we need to be alone, take your time getting here."

"What happen?" Tommy whispered as he went into his office.

"Thomas I've been snorting cocaine and Alisha found my stash this morning." Julian whispered as he hid in the bathroom within the room.

"This is too deep to talk about now, I'll see you later." Tommy said shaking his head he hung up.

He sat down to think, Julian looked at me and said, "Alisha do you need..." The doctor rushed in after the nurse informed her that my water broke. "Let's go this baby's crowning" Julian ran to hold my hand as the nurses scrambled to get me into position. Before the doctor could tell me to push my baby boy was out and crying. "Congratulations," the doctor said as she handed the baby to Julian. He looked down through tears and said "You want to meet mommy." As Julian held our son all the anger I had subsided and I kissed him. The nurse took the baby to finish cleaning him up. Julian quickly exclaimed with watered eyes, "Alisha please don't leave me I won't do it again."

I reached for his hand. "Julian that's not important right now" I replied as I closed my eyes to rest. "Let's just enjoy this moment." I squeezed his hand to reassure him.

Tommy came rushing in forty-five minutes later. "Alisha, how are you" he asked searching for his next breath.

I sat up puzzled and asked, "Tommy why are you out of breath?"

He leaned over and between each breath he replied, "I ran from the parking deck and up the stairs because I was late getting here."

I beckoned him over as Julian walked into the room. Julian looking puzzled because Tommy was bent over as if he had been punched in the belly. "Hey Tommy, when did you get here?"

Having caught his breath he replied, "A few minutes ago." Tommy walked over to the bed and kissed me on the forehead, "How are you feeling?"

I smiled, "Tommy I'm good." I began to rub his arm.

Julian walked to the other side of the bed and said, "Alisha I told Tommy that you asked for a divorce and why." His eyes pleaded for forgiveness and reassurance. "That's okay Julian I would've told him anyway." I said with a lack of expression. "Do you want a divorce?" Julian and Tommy exclaimed in unison.
I looked between both of them and slid down into the covers. "I don't know." Julian stepped back as tears that would only fall down one cheek entered his eyes and Tommy's mouth fell open but no sound followed as he blinked his eyes in disbelief. Julian walked out and Tommy walked out behind him while I turned over in a confused state unsure of what to do.

Moments later Tommy walked back into the room. "Alisha, are you really going to give up on your husband?"
I looked up at him "No but I have a right to be upset and he has an obligation to work for my forgiveness." I said pouting
Tommy shook his head "I know you're not going to be like that you spoiled woman."
I faked a shocked look before smiling and becoming serious. "Tommy if he had cheated I could forgive him but he is using illegal drugs and he started after we got married."

"Wait you could forgive him for cheating but not drugs." He said looking puzzled.

"Yes Tommy because I understand why good, heck great men cheat but drugs I don't get." I looked around the room and motioned for Tommy to come closer before saying, "Tommy I can compete with another woman but I can't compete with the satisfaction he gets from drugs."

Tommy turned and laughed until he was doubled over. I was pouting and had folded my arms when he walked to the bed gently pulling my hand into his and said, "So this is about your sick ego." Tommy sat on the bed. "Baby it's time to completely let go of that part of you because you have so much more to offer than your skills in the bed. Alisha being with you is better than being in you any day but until you realize that you are settling for less and offering less than you're worth" Tommy kissed me on the forehead as tears ran down my face because I knew he was right. I had not let go of my clean-up woman attitude because it was my security blanket and I was scared to trust God completely but the revelation didn't hit me until Tommy said it. I repented in my mind and leaned back as I pondered the truth of that revelation I fell asleep.

Julian walked into the room thirty minutes later Tommy jumped up and whispered, "Man where have you been?" "I took a drive." He said calmly. Looking around he continued. "I was thinking about my actions and how I hurt my wife." Julian stepped into the hallway. "Where are you going Julian?" Tommy asked looking puzzled. Julian walked into the room pulling a cart full of flowers, candy, and an assortment of stuffed animals. Tommy exclaimed showing his annoyance, "Do you really think this is going to rectify the issue in your marriage?"
Julian smiled and said, "No but it will soften her up."

I awake rubbing my eyes. "What's going on you guys?" Julian ran to the side of my bed with a big stupid grin holding bear. "Julian what are you doing?" I asked sitting up "You know I don't like that stuff." Tommy laughed and gave Julian the told you so look as he turned to get a box of candy. "Is this better?" Julian asked with an even bigger smile.
"You know it is." I said smiling as I grabbed the box ripping it open.
Tommy shook his head. "Alisha you are sad." He said as he laughed.
Julian laughed, "Leave my greedy baby

alone unless she gains weight." That statement caused a hush in the room. Julian quickly replied, "Baby I'm clean and I signed up for treatment." He grabbed my hand and with pleading eyes he said. "I'm never going to touch the stuff again."

"So when are we going to take the DNA test?" I asked remembering his statement and why.

"I told you it wasn't necessary but we can do it today if that's what you want." He said shaking his head.

"Julian do you know how many women have had another man's baby but the man thinks it's his?"

"No and I'm sure you don't either." He laughed.

Tommy held up one finger and tipped out the door which caused me to laugh and refocus.

"Julian, when do you start rehab?" I asked. "I go tonight baby." He said squeezing my hand.

"How long will you be in Julian?" I asked. He squeezed my hand to reassure me.

"Alisha it could be two weeks or two months depending on my progress but you know that."

I rolled my eyes and snatched my hand away. "You have put an unnecessary strain on this marriage and our family." I looked

at him with tears in my eyes. "Julian just because you get clean does not mean our relationship will go back to normal."
He started rubbing his face and let out a deep sigh before saying, "I know but we have to start somewhere." He kissed my forehead.
"I want you to understand I won't visit you." I pouted and folded my arm like a child. I knew that if this was a patient I would encourage a different attitude from their loved ones. Not giving support during his time of need was selfish on my part and I had to work out this anger before it turned into a bigger issue.
"Baby I understand." He sadly replied as he laid his head next to mine.

A couple of days later we left the hospital. Tommy came to pick us up. Ms. Daniels had to take care of Millie because Julian was in rehab and I was in the hospital.

New Life

As we were driving I realized Tommy was going the wrong way. "Hey Tommy that is not the way to my house," I said looking around.

"Yes it is." he replied looking straight ahead.

"Tommy I know where I live." I exclaimed.

"Apparently not," he sarcastically replied.

By the time we finished with the back and forth we pulled up into the driveway of the new house. Tommy parked the car and said, "Julian wanted to be here to carry you over the threshold to your new beginning but..."

He was cut short when my door swung open and I looked up into the man I loved face "Julian!" I cried as he picked me up out of the car and carried me in to the house.

Julian whispered in my ear, "Baby this is the start of a new day." I smiled and kissed him as he slowly put me down.

"Okay, okay that's enough you guys need to

wait until we leave." Tommy joked as he walked into the house with the baby.

I looked around and asked, "Where is Millie?"

Suddenly I heard a scream, "Mommy Mommy." Millie came running in and bear hugged my legs causing me to stumble so I reached down picked her up spun her around.

"Put her down." Tommy commanded as Julian reached for her she began to cry.

I looked sad and ran to sit down so Julian could place her on my lap. With all of the excitement of everyone seeing the house for the first time they forgot about the baby. Tommy looked around, "So Julian are you going to give us a tour?"

Julian jumped when he was asked the question because his focus was on me. "Yes yes come on." Everyone followed him throughout the house. I talked to Millie as we stayed behind to have some alone time and I introduce her to her little brother Julian or Lil J as she demanded.

When everyone came back Millie was playing in my hair and I asked, "How was the tour?"

Tommy exclaimed, "It was nice Lisha, y'all have a beautiful home."

"Thank you Thomas." Julian said.

I smiled as I stood up and said, "Well I guess it time for Julian to take his family around." He smiled and picked up Millie as I picked up the baby. He took us to the baby's room first so we could lay him down. The next room was Millie's and she jumped up and down yelling, "That's me that's me." She pointed to the painting of her on the wall opposite the window and to the right of her bed. He had created a dream princess room for her. He lead us to Little Julian's future room which was incomplete before leading me down the hall opening the double doors of the corridor leading to our bedroom. "Oh my Julian," I turned to him still covering my mouth. "This is beautiful." I said in awe. The corridor leading to the bedroom was covered with wall paintings of us throughout the years on the right. To the left were separate walk-in closets with black and white photos of us and the closet had shoe racks from the floor to the ceiling. When I walked into our room I was astonished our bed was round with a mirror over the bed and a separate sitting area with a fire place. He took me into a room to the left of the sitting area and I held my stomach laughing because it was a room with a mini bar, two tables, and a stage with a pole. "Julian my freaky love you know me so well." I said passionately kissing him until he was at full attention. He escorted me throughout the room before ending with the bathroom. As I pushed him out of the bathroom. I thought it resembled the spa we were married at so I walked back back into the bathroom. "I have a great husband so I'm going to support him better." I yelled. When I stepped into the amazing shower my anger melted away for good. Twenty minutes later I was dressed and ready for bed. Julian the baby is sleeping in here with us tonight." I said as I finished putting on lotion.

"Alisha I'm not staying." He said slowly

I spun around in anger and shouted, "What?"

He walked over to me and put his arms around me saying, "Baby I will be there for at least another two weeks or so." Julian gently kissed me on the forehead and held me tighter before he continued, "Alisha I know the pain I've caused was unnecessary but at the time I felt a great inadequacy."

I squeezed my husband tightly around his waist as tears fell from my eyes. "Julian I'm sorry for not supporting you during your worst moment." Stepping back and looking him in his eyes I said, "Baby you are all the man I need and we will beat this thing together."

He smiled as all doubt faded and whispered

in my ear, "I know you were disappointed with my actions and I will always be honest with you from this day forward." After his confession I loosened his pants and dropped with them as I pulled him closer. I caressed my husband with my superb expertise and his legs became weak so he dropped to the floor giving in to the pleasure.

"Baby you know I can't handle that now how do you expect me to leave." He announced trying to pull himself together. "Yes I do Julian." I said as I hopped to my feet. "Julian it's been a few days and I don't know when I'll see you again so I had to hook you up."

He got up and zipped his pants saying, "Alisha I know you love me and would never betray me but after losing you the first time I refused to lose you again." We kissed and he walked out the door for what seemed like years.

Julian had some deep secrets and insecurities that he never told me about until after his recovery. I knew he had some issue that he didn't want to face but never new how deep it went. Julian was considered to be that man every woman dreamed of having so he freely gave of himself until he met the woman of his dreams. Rasheda hurt him in several ways which caused a greater need to prove his manhood. This is the mistake some men make instead of accepting who they are they need to prove something to the world and that becomes their focus; which causes a greater psychological damage not only to them but those who love and accept them as they are. Julian had lost a sense of control over his life, his manhood, and a belief in himself because he thought I walked out of his life because of his quick draw. Rasheda, his first love, cheating on him caused him to wonder if he could satisfy a woman. Julian had never looked at his actions or lack of communication as the real issue for the failure in his marriage because pointing fingers and holding his true feeling inside was his solution.

During that time I missed my husband but Ms. Daniels, Ma Carrie, and Tommy made sure I didn't get overwhelmed. Since I had given up my clinic and merged it with the Steinberg Community Center which consisted of a daycare center, basketball court, nutrition and exercise classes, counseling center and an educational center for all ages my second house was now my office. I finally gave up my practice to help other beginning Therapist and

Psychologists but they had to volunteer at least twenty hours a month. We had people volunteer their services year-round to help in different areas; the daycare was the only hired staff. Julian wanted me to stop working so I did. I had several sources of income in which I worked hard to start but now it was time to sit back and reap the benefits of that labor which started when I was sixteen. Papa always told me to own something besides a house so we opened a towing company next to his garage and it grew in that small town to four garages and over eighty employees. Tobias towing and garage was given to me when I turned twenty-one but Papa ran the company until he was tired. I could sell it after he passed but I let Uncle Junior oversee the company until Millie was born and I sold a portion of the company to him so I still reaped the benefits. Deuces, Charles's son, took over after I sat down in the construction business but I still had more than half the ownership of that company so I reap those benefits. I rented the rooms out; which I made into individual offices, at my old clinic. The center is a Non-profit program ran by a board and I'm on that board. I was recently approached to give seminars as a counselor and motivational speaker to encourage the youth and young college students four times a year. I'm financially stable and my husband is rich so I think it's time to sit down and enjoy our life.

A few weeks after I got home I received a text from Mikael letting me know he was in town and wanted to have dinner so I called Tommy. "Hey Tommy how are you?"
"Hey Alisha what's up?" he asked with suspicion in his voice so I came clean.
"Mikael is in town and wants to..."
"So what does that have to do with you?" He said annoyed.
"Tommy, come on." I said smiling. "I want you to..."
"No and I don't believe Julian would like it either." He said with a little as a matter of fact in his tone.
"Tommy, Julian trusts me and he's not here so I called you." I said trying to kiss up but to no avail.
"Alisha I know what you're doing and no!" he exclaimed and hung up.

Tommy didn't like Mikael because of what he did to cause our break-up but I had forgiven Mikael and wanted to resolve our issues. I text Mikael to let him know I would meet them tonight at eight for dinner. I hadn't seen Mikael since that day at my office and the issues surrounding him storming out of my house had not been resolved but we would text and he sent those familiar boxes until I told him I married Julian. It was almost seven and I had changed clothes eight times before I decided on the perfect outfit. We were meeting at Aerials Delicacy because we both loved to eat there and he is the reason the owner became my client. I got there around seven forty-five and Mikael was waiting for me at the door.

"Hello Alisha, how are you?" he asked as he hugged me.

"I'm well and you?" I said as he released me from his embrace.

"I am well finally." He proudly said stepping back and putting his arm around a woman that resembled me. "Alisha I would like you to meet my spiritual wife Faith." I smiled and leaned in to give her a hug but she stuck out her hand. "It is so nice to finally meet you Faith." After we introduced ourselves Jack walked up with his Life partner Jerri. Jerri screamed, "Alisha when I found out you would be here tonight I had to come and see you." We talked as we were escorted to a private dining area and I gave him my card as we parted ways. Jerri was 6' tall with a slim muscular build and deep voice. He was a high end decorator, event coordinator, and personal stylist. Jack was 5'9" muscular but thick, soft spoken, and quiet but owned three high end restaurants. They had been together for twenty years and bought a house in another state so they could get married and live there after retirement.

After we were seated I could see that Faith was uncomfortable so I focused my attention on her. "Faith, how long have you guys been married?" I asked knowing the answer and pondering my next question. "Six months." She nervously replied. Holding her head down causing me to give up by the time the waitress brought us our drinks and took our order. After the waitress walked away Mikael and I started talking about Papa and the things he would say. I realized Papa and Mikael's relationship was deeper than I thought. We had forgotten Faith was there by the time we had gotten to dessert. After the waitress took a carryout order and walked away Faith yelled out, "I'm having his child so you can't have him back." Tears rolled down her cheeks as Mikael and I looked at each other in confusion. Mikael kneeled next to her whispering in her ear she nodded and regained her composure. She softly said, "Forgive me Alisha for disrespecting you." She folded her hands in her lap and held her head down.

"There is no need to apologize Faith and congratulations." I quickly replied wishing I had listened to Tommy.

"Yes she does." Mikael abruptly replied. I smiled and praised God silently for dodging that bullet but what could have changed him or was he always like this and love blinded me from the truth. Grams always said, "When a mate is removed from your life it might be God's blessing of protection. Dinner ended quickly and we said our good-byes as we parted ways.

On the ride home I wondered why Mikael had become so bitter. My thoughts were interrupted by my ringing phone. "Hello" "Alisha this is...." the phone cut off I looked at my phone and I had a signal. When I approached the light I looked at the call log but the name and number was blocked. I thought the person may have called the wrong number but they said my name. I was so entrenched in my thoughts I didn't realize where I was going and it didn't click until I opened the front door. Out of habit I drove to our first home and the memories of all the good times Julian and I had flooded my mind. I sat on the sofa and cried as I prayed for my husband. I leaned back after I prayed and had peace for the first time since this mess started. As I enjoyed the peace and memories the doorbell rang. I thought "Who could this be?" I went to the door and to my surprise it was...

"Hello Alisha." He said with a smile and pleading eyes. I could not believe my eyes but I regained my thoughts and replied, "What are you doing here?"

Looking around he quickly asked with a nervous under tone, "Can we talk?"

I stepped outside and pulled the door up. "Yes." I said emotionless.

"How are you?" he asked with a nervous smile.

"I'm great but how did you find me?" I asked sternly.

"I looked you up on the internet after I saw you moved out of the other house." He leaned back on the railing. "I hope you're not upset with me." He calmly said.

I was still sexually attracted to him so I had to maintain my focus. "No but I'm married so please don't pop up at my house." I said with annoyance.

"I'm sorry Alisha but I've been here three times and I haven't seen anyone so I called but lost my nerve." He said in that looking for sympathy tone he does so well.

"I just had a baby so I've been staying with a friend while my husband went on a business trip." I lied with confidence.

He slowly walked over to me. "Alisha I will

never stop loving you." He gently pulled my hand to his lips and softly kissed my fingertips. "I know you don't cheat so I will respect that but I'll never give up on us because you are my soul mate and we belong together." He turned went to his car and drove away. I had become sexually aroused and felt guilty because in my mind I had cheated on Julian so I gathered myself and went home. After I got home I washed the stench and betrayal of that moment off me and prayed before I went to bed.

Tommy came over extra early the next morning. "Wake up sleepy head." He said opening the curtains but it was still dark outside so he cut on the lamp. "I know you got in late because I didn't see your car before I went to bed." He walked over to the bed shaking me until he saw my eyes. He slowly rolled me over and with fear in his voice he asked, "What happened last night?"
"I don't want to talk about last night." He jumped and angrily asked, "What did Mikael do to you this time?" Before I could answer he questioned me again, "Did you have sex with him Alisha?"
"Tommy no it's not Mikael." I yelled as I got up, "It was someone else."

"Wait how did... When did you... Who was it?" he exclaimed

I flopped down on the bed. "Tommy I went to the old house and the thoughts of Julian overwhelmed me until the doorbell rang."

Tommy said in disgust, "How could you Alisha?"

"Tommy I didn't meet him he found out where the house was and just showed up."

Tommy didn't believe me. "Why would he just show up and why were you there?"

"I had so much on my mind after dinner I just drove home out of habit."

"Alisha I'm no fool you allowed Mikael to trick you into bed because you're still mad at Julian." He said in disappointment.

"Mikael is married and they are having their first child so I was alone." I said annoyed.

"I'm sorry Lisha but why were you at the house?" his disgust turned into concern.

"Out of habit and when I walked in I thought about what Julian and I shared." Tears fell as I spoke remembering the feelings from last night.

"When did Mikael come over and did he hurt you?" Tommy asked with a nervous guilt.

"No he just wanted me to know he had moved on and was happy."

"What does that mean and why are you sad about it?" Tommy asked looking puzzled

I sighed heavily and said, "I don't know or care." I got up to get breakfast ready.

"Where are you going Alisha?" Tommy asked

"Down stairs to make the kids breakfast." He rushed out to my closet. "No you're not I'm taking the new mommy's to breakfast so get dressed." He peeked out and said, "This closet is bigger than our bedroom."

"Tommy we live a few houses down from each other so how could that be?"

"Your husband had more money than I did." We laughed as I ushered him out so I could get dressed. After I got dressed I took Lil J to Ms. Daniels and kissed Millie on the head. "Ms. Daniels I will take the kids for the rest of the day so you can take some time off."

"Child I don't have anything to do but take care of these babies, so enjoy your day." She said shooing me off.

Ms. Daniels and her daughter had a big disagreement over a year ago and she banned her from seeing her grandchildren. We offered her legal help but she refused our assistance and focused her attention on Millie and now Lil J. I felt awful but I had to respect her wishes so I let her spend all the time she wanted with the kids; even taking her with us on my alone time with Millie.

Tommy and Isabella were waiting in the car for me so when I got to the car Tommy jumped out and opened the rear passenger door for me. "Where are we going Tommy?" I said as I buckled my seat belt.

Isabella responded first. "He won't tell it's a surprise."

"Yes it's a surprise for our wives." He said smiling.

I thought that he was picking up Julian or meeting him somewhere so I became excited.

"Why are you smiling so hard Alisha?" Tommy asked looking at me in the rear view mirror.

"Yes Alisha why?" Isabella chimed in.

I replied a little giddy, "Nothing just thinking about Julian and breakfast." I sat back and closed my eyes. They would include me from time to time in their conversation until they realized I was not responding they continued without me. Tommy and Isabella chatted until we arrived at our destination.

Tommy walked to the door and put in a code and opened the door before he escorted us out of the car. Isabella was amazed and lost herself in the beauty of the Cabana as she disappeared into the bathroom. I walked in with a big smile because I knew it was a surprise but my heart sank when I didn't see Julian and as tears rose in my eyes I asked, "Tommy how did you get this room?"

Tommy embraced me when he saw my face saying, "Alisha what's wrong?"

I buried my face in his chest crying, "I thought Julian was going to be here."

Pulling me away from himself he said, "Lisha I'm sorry Julian told me about this place a few months ago so I got an account." He walked me into one of the bedrooms. "Alisha I want you to get some rest while we order brunch."

"Tommy will you get me the French toast."

Tommy smiled and walked out as I closed my eyes quickly falling asleep in the mist of disappointment.

Moments later the door opened and through closed eyes I said, "Tommy, give me five more minutes." I snuggled into the pillow to continue my peaceful rest. The door closed and Tommy snuggled up in the bed next to me. "Tommy we can't do this anymore because we're married and it doesn't look right." I tried to move but he kissed me on the neck so I jumped up and screamed, "Tommy what the..." But as I looked into his eyes I melted sitting back down on the bed he pulled me closer for a passionate kiss. "I see you missed that." He chuckled as he pushed me back on the bed he slowly pulled up my dress causing me to moan with expectation. He pulled my panties off so I arched my back to raise myself up off the bed. I caressed his head as he kissed my thighs and with each kiss he moaned, "I've missed your scent and the softness of you Alisha." Slowly he buried his throbbing manhood into the warmness of my pleasure causing me to scream out and pull him closer. He whispered in my ear, "I've missed you so much baby." As he continued to whisper his thoughts and feelings in my ear as his thrust became harder and deeper causing me to release my essence. Feeling the wetness he exploded returning the result of total pleasure. He rolled over taking quick short breaths he said, "I've missed you in every way."

"I've missed you too." I said as I snuggled under him.

"Baby girl I've missed you more than you'll ever know." He said kissing me on the forehead. "Come on let's go eat something." We cleaned up and got dressed before going into the other room to eat.

Tommy had a big goofy smile as we walk out of the room. "I see your attitude has changed Alisha." He exclaimed.

"Yes it has." I replied holding Julian's arm for dear life.

"Baby I'm home for good now so you can loosen the Kung Fu grip." He laughed. I smiled as he pulled out my chair so I could sit down. We enjoyed our brunch that had turned into a late lunch because of the reunion.

"When did you leave the facility Julian?" I asked.

"Last night baby." He said looking at Tommy as he quickly looked down.

"So I take it you know about me going out with Mikael last night." I asked looking at the top of Tommy's head because he never looked up.

"Yes I do but we can talk about your actions later." He said taking a sip of his drink.

"It's great to see you Julian." Isabella blurted out.

"Yes it is we've missed you man and the golf course keeps calling your name." Tommy chimed in causing laughter from everyone except m.e

I didn't know what Tommy had told Julian and I was upset with my so called best friend. When Tommy finally looked up with pleading eyes he mouthed, "I'm sorry" but I rolled my eyes and got up from the table.

"Hey beautiful where are you going?" Julian said softly as he grabbed my hand.

"I'm going to the bathroom." I said with a smile.

Tommy yelled out nervously, "I'm sorry Alisha I thought you were going to dinner alone with Mikael." He was giving me a heads up on what he told Julian but I was so upset I didn't get it.

Julian stood up and embraced me. "Baby lets go in the other room to talk." Julian squeezed my hand slightly and we walked into the bedroom.

As I sat on the bed Julian sat next to me, putting his arm around me he said, "Why did you go out with Mikael last night?"

I looked Julian in his eyes as I said, "To meet his new wife."

"Wait what....I thought you were going on a date." He said puzzled.

"I did but it was a double date and Tommy wouldn't go so I went alone." I said and fell back on the bed. Julian stood up and started pacing the floor and scratched his head before he said another word he looked up at the ceiling.

"Tell me what happened last night."

"Last night I went to dinner with Mikael

and his spiritual wife, Faith." I said sitting up. "She was upset because Mikael and I got along so well." I continued as I stood up "But the surprise was when Malcolm came over." I put my head on Julian's chest. Julian yelled as he pushed me back by my shoulders, "How did he find our house?" Holding Julian's hand I said, "Not the new house but the one we just moved from." He snatched away from me and with a demanding tone asked, "What were you doing there?"

"Julian calm down." I said rushing closer to embrace him.

"I went there out of habit because I was thinking about the good times we had." I watched his face soften as I continued. "I was sitting in the living room reminiscing when Malcolm knocked on the door and asked me to..."

"Wait a minute Malcolm how did he find the house, does he want you back but you guys haven't had any contact in almost a year." Julian looked at me suspiciously. "I want a DNA test because something isn't right."

"Julian we can do that Monday." I said as I sat down.

"Wait, that's it no yelling or tears." He said walking over to me.

"Julian how long have you known me, right so you should know I wouldn't get upset." I looked up at him before I continued, "I know it's because of the actions of your first wife." I said and lay back on the bed.

Julian lay down next to me and held me as he started kissing me on my head and cheeks. "Baby I'm sorry but I know how you felt about Malcolm and the sexual experience was amazing to you which doesn't matter because you want me."
I threw my arms around his neck and gave him a big kiss saying "We are still getting a DNA test Monday and I've loved you more than any man I've ever met." As soon as I started to unbutton his pants Tommy knocked on the door. "Man what!" Julian yelled.
"It's time to head back." He said through the door. We got up and walked out the room. Is everything ok?" Tommy asked.
"Yes Thomas, Alisha and I are good." Julian said. I smiled as he pulled me closer.
We got in the car and drove home filling the car with laughter and conversation on the ride home.

When we got home Julian went straight for the kids. Millie ran to him before he got in the door good yelling, "DJ Daddy J I missed you." She jumped up in his arms. "Hi mommy." She said waving at me over his shoulder.

"Hello Millie." I said as I picked up Lil J. Julian played with Millie until she made us come in the play room and watch her favorite movie. We sat on the sofa and watched the movie. Ms. Daniels went to sit with Ma Carrie for a spell, as Ma Carrie would say.

Arrangement

Early Saturday morning my phone rang.
"Hello"
"Alisha it's me I'm on my way over."
"Ok." I hung up and got dressed before I woke
up Millie to dress her. I was excited about her
going to see Alonzo but Julian was a little
uncomfortable. He had grown close to Millie and
didn't want to share the daddy role he had alone
for almost a year.

Millie was in her usual position waiting so
when Mr. Avery's car pulled up in the driveway
Millie started screaming, "Papa Papa." We didn't
tell her Alonzo was with him. When I walked to
the door and opened it for her and Alonzo was
standing in the doorway. Millie let out the
biggest scream and jumped in his arms. "Daddy
I missed you." She screamed as she hugged his
neck. When Julian and Mr. Avery met they hit it
off so well they played golf together. Millie was
still hugging Alonzo when I walked in with
Julian. "Hello Alonzo." I said and when we
looked into each other's eyes everyone in the
room could see what we quickly tried to hide.

"Daddy, get my bags." Millie screamed causing the room to refocus. "Alonzo this is Julian my husband." I said quickly averting my eyes. I became uncomfortable because I still loved Alonzo and I could see he felt the same. Julian and Alonzo shook hands and were cordial but Mr. Avery and Julian greeted like old friends and refocused the room again. As he and Mr. Avery talked Alonzo and I talked about Millie's upcoming birthday party. Alonzo whispered, "Is that your golf buddy?"

"Yes."

"So my mom was right when she said you were cheating."

"No because we didn't have sex until after we were married and I started seeing him after the party."

"Am I supposed to believe that Alisha?"

"That's your choice." I said walking back into the foyer.

When it was time to go Millie grabbed Julian's hand and said, "Come on DJ let's go." I picked up Millie and said, "No baby you're going with Daddy and Papa but Julian has to stay here with us."

Millie pouted, "But I want my daddy to play with DJ."

We all laughed. Julian whispered in Millie's ear causing her to jump down and run to Alonzo. Alonzo looked at me with pleading eyes that were full of pain. As tears came to my eyes I walked over and kissed Millie on the cheek and ran upstairs. Julian had already walked out with Mr. Avery to put Millie's things in the car. When they drove off Julian came upstairs in the baby's room where I was changing his diaper.

"Are you okay?" He asked

"Yes." I smiled never looking up. "Why would you ask me that?"

"Your daughter will be gone for a month and you're not upset?" He asked putting his arms around me and kissing my neck.

"Yes I'm a little sad but that's her daddy and he hasn't seen her in almost a year." I sighed and put the baby in his bed.

"Alisha that man is still in love with you." He said losing his cool

"Julian I knew that was why you came up here you were concerned about me and Alonzo." I said looking for the babies clothes.

"Yes I'm a little concern because I could see it in his eyes even when he looked away." He said as he picked the baby up.

"What are you doing Alisha?" Ms. Daniels said rushing in

"I'm getting my little man dressed so I can feed him." I said puzzled.

"Well you have a meeting with the planner for Millie's party in less than fifteen minutes." She retorted.

I kissed the baby and ran out the room with Julian right behind me saying, "I'll drive."

As soon as we drove off the questions started.
"So Alisha do you want him back?"
Annoyed I said, "Julian you go out with Rasheda
all the time and I don't say a word."
"But that's different."
"How is it different?"
"I'm not in love with her but I saw how you
looked at Alonzo."
"Julian I haven't seen the man in almost a year
so yes I was taken back a little."
"So should I be concerned?"
"No, Julian because you are my husband and
I'm crazy mad in love with you my soul mate the
man that makes my heart leap." I kissed the
back of his hand and he smiled like a Cheshire
cat. "I can't wait to see her face next weekend."
He cheered changing the subject "Me either."

When we pulled up Dawn was getting out of
her car on the phone. "Hey guys I'll be with you
in a minute." Julian and I walked into the office.
The receptionist was always extremely bubbly.
"Hello Alisha who's the model?"
"Hi Tina this is my husband Julian."
"Where's Thomas?" she said waiting for Julian's
response to her question.
"I guess he's at home with his wife, Isabella." I
said a little disappointed with her actions.
"How is he?" she asked looking at Julian as if he
was a piece of meat and she was starving. I was
about to ask her a question when Dawn,

Julian's cousin, walked in. "Put your tongue back in your mouth and stop disrespecting my cousin." She said hugging me and rolling her eyes at Julian. She knew he was a womanizer when they were younger so she thought he started the flirting. "So my cousin is having a party for his baby." Julian smiled because he was so proud. "Put your chest back in pretty boy it's because you finally picked the right woman you're standing her so respect her." Julian pulled me closer, "Always"
She smacked as she rolled her eyes, "humph"
I laughed, "He is innocent she was flirting with him." Julian looked confused because he rarely noticed other woman if I were around now if he was alone that's a different story. We went into her office to approve the final plans.

The weekend of Millie's party Alonzo, Ginger and his parents came. I tried to avoid eye contact because we didn't want to hurt Julian. Ginger made it a point to show me her ring and tell me about the wedding date, but all I notice was that the ring was extremely small and the date was a year away. Julian was right behind me whenever I got close to Alonzo and Alonzo stared at me the whole day. Millie ran around like she had lost her mind. Alonzo's mother kept trying to stop her from running so she would hold her but his father would help her down so she could have fun with the other kids.

When it was time to sing "Happy Birthday" Ginger held on to Alonzo for dear life and tried to convince him not to stand next to Millie. Mr. Avery walked up to me. "Alisha my son is miserable and he's still in love with you."
"Mr. Avery I'm married so I can't acknowledge that." I smiled and walked away glancing back at Alonzo. I became nervous because I wanted Julian and him to build a relationship for Millie's sake but Alonzo stared at me as if he didn't care who knew. Tommy walked over to Alonzo and started a conversation. Tommy later invited Julian and they looked like old friends within minutes. I was relieved. Ginger hated me and never missed the opportunity to show it so she and Mrs. Avery sat off to themselves and gave nasty looks during the party. Millie did not like Ginger and would cry or run whenever she came around so Alonzo spent time with Millie alone or with his parents. He had taken a month off but would start traveling again going back and forth overseas heading different projects for the next year. That's why the wedding day was postponed or at least that was the excuse. I walked over to the three men and Julian grabbed me kissing me on the cheek. "I hope you guys are having fun."
"Yes we are Le Le." Alonzo said "Our baby is growing up so fast."
Tommy chimed in after seeing Julian's face and Alonzo gaze. "Yeah, Lisha we are and it's good to

catch up with old friends and introduce new ones."

Julian laughed. "Baby I think that's Thomas's polite way of saying leave and let us men enjoy ourselves." I patted my husband's arm and walked away. Alonzo and Julian watched me until I walked into the house, while Tommy fearful of Julian catching Alonzo watching me sweated. Julian and Tommy decided to sneak off and play golf after the party so they invited Alonzo. I was glad because this was the start of a new relationship. The party was over and I was glad. Millie put herself to bed an hour after the party. She was sleep until it was time for her to go home with Alonzo.

After the month was over Alonzo asked if we could set up an arrangement for Millie to spend time with him on a regular basis. We met at our favorite restaurant which was owned by his good friend. We set up a schedule and made plans about Millie but after we walked outside the conversation got deeper. "Alisha I would like to thank you for respecting me as Millie's father."

I was a little puzzled. "What do you mean?"

He took a deep breath, "I was rude, called you out of your name, and accused you of things but you never said a bad thing about me to Millie."

"That would be wrong."

"I know" he held his head down for a moment

before holding it up to reveal something to me. I told him, "Come on let's sit in my car and finish talking." We sat in my car for over two hours talking and he revealed some things to me about his issues with his father that was being worked out. Ginger told him that Mr. Avery was not his biological father and most of the details from Ginger were not true but when he saw the time his dad took up with Millie he had to sit down and talked with him. Ginger kept calling while we talked but he wouldn't answer, she called every fifteen minutes and after the fourth call he stopped responding. Julian text me but was okay with the situation once he knew we were in a public place. "Alisha I want to say I'm sorry and you were right. My mom never called you that day and she did try to break us up so I could be with Ginger." "That's how it should be Alonzo I expect people to think higher of their mother than other people even when their mother is foul because that's human nature."

"Alisha I love you but I'm starting to care a great deal about Ginger and she wants to start a family." Alonzo just stopped talking and got out of the car. He got into his car and drove off.

When Alonzo got home Ginger was waiting for him in his driveway. She jumped out of the car when he pulled up. When he got out she screamed, "So was she worth it?" Alonzo got back into his car and drove off. Ginger didn't have a key to his house, was not allowed to come over without calling, and he would only let her satisfy him orally with a condom that he would remove tie up and flush after they were done. He didn't trust Ginger and he didn't like the fact she was always trying to pull him away from Millie or that Millie was scared of Ginger. When he was with Millie he would not allow Ginger to call or come over. Ginger and his mom were always cooking up plots but his dad would inform him of their plans. Ginger wanted to trap Alonzo and his mother wanted her to do it by having kids.

When I got home Julian ran to meet me at the door. "Julian what's wrong with you?" I knew what the issue was but I played dumb. "Nothing I just missed you come on let's go upstairs."
"Can I see my kids first?"
"They are sleep." Julian picked me up and carried me upstairs.
"Let me take a shower first." I said trying to pull off my clothes as I walked to the bathroom.
"No." he said blocking my way "I want the muskiness of the day on you."
I looked at him sideways "Have you lost your mind?"
"No baby I just want you."
So I pulled up my skirt and lay out in the floor.

Julian dropped between my legs and jumped back up, "I don't smell anything and where are your panties."

I smiled "That's right I took a shower before I left the hotel and my..." I started laughing but Julian started cursing and pulled out his phone. "Julian I was joking I took off my panties first." I opened my hand and he snatched them. "Why the hell you smell like you just got out of the shower?"

"I used the wipes by the door that I told you to put up last night."

"You are not funny"

"No but I'm not a cheater and you should trust me." I started laughing again as he went to the sitting area to sulk. "Baby I'm going down stairs to see our children."

"Hi Ms. Daniels, how are you?"

"Child I'm glad you're home that man like to drove me crazy worrying about you and you know who." She said pointing with her eyes to Millie so I wouldn't say a name. I sat down and played with the kids for a few moments and got up to start dinner. Julian came down stairs with my phone in his hand. "Why is he calling you, hasn't he talked to you enough?"

"Yes we talked but something could've happened." I said grabbing the phone to call him back. "Hey Alonzo is everything good with you?"

"Yes I was calling to see if we could be friends

and reconnect what we had before we started an intimate relationship?"

"That's cool with me but I'm in the middle of dinner so I'll talk to you tomorrow."

"Bye Alisha."

Before I could hang up the phone good Julian started asking questions, "What did he want?"

"Julian we can go upstairs later and we can talk."

When we got into our room I started talking. "Julian when you go see your kids Rasheda is always there and sometimes she forgets to bring them. You have met her in hotels, she's put lipstick on your shirt, and scratch marks on your neck but I don't say a word because I trust you. You came home two days ago and screwed me because she turned you on but you don't trust me. Julian I never put myself in a compromising position but you do every time you meet her so unless you are doing the do when you meet your ex don't ever question my relationship or actions with Alonzo." I folded my arms because I was done.

"I hate being married to a woman who can slick talk better than me you make me sick." We burst in to laughter. "I will treat y'all to dinner to the rest of the week since I was wrong and want to keep the peace."

"Great so what are you cooking?"

"The catering company will tell me." He laughed

"I should've known." I kissed my husband on his forehead and we returned to our kids. When we got down stairs Ms. Daniels looked up at us and chuckled. I smiled and Julian said, "Ms. Daniels that's not funny. After we ate dinner and put the kids to bed. Julian decided he wanted a stripper that night so I gave him a show, a special in the bar, and we went to bed.

Early one morning Julian ran off to play golf after we had sex. The men started to build a strong relationship over the next few months because Mr. Avery, Julian, Tommy, and Alonzo played at least twice a week together, when Alonzo was in town. The women on the other hand didn't. When Ginger would go out with us on couple dates she would roll her eyes at me constantly and question Alonzo on our whereabouts or the time we spent on the phone trying to upset Julian. We decided to invite Alonzo without Ginger after the third couples date. We went on family outing that Ginger and Mrs. Avery were never invited to because Ginger scared Millie and Mrs. Avery would tell Ginger where we were so she could pop up. The bond we built was strong and we parented the kids like a village. Alonzo decided to ease away from Ginger causing his relationship with his mom was shaky.

A few months later Ginger announced she was pregnant which devastated Alonzo. He called me so I rushed to his house not knowing what had happened to him. When I got there I opened the door without thinking with my key. Alonzo was passed out drunk in his living room. "Alonzo," I cried out to him as I picked up his bottles. He moaned and cursed but I couldn't make out what he was saying. I helped him up and walked him to the couch. Alonzo sat up and fell back over. I had called Tommy and Julian before I got there so Julian would know I was there just in case he heard a different story. I went into the kitchen and made him some coffee when Tommy called me back and told me he was on the way. When I came in the living room Ginger was standing there. "Bitch he's mine now."

"Ginger he called me crying and the phone cut off so I didn't know what was going on."

You're a lie you want Alonzo back."

"Ginger I assure you I wouldn't give Julian up for the world."

Julian walked into the room with a big smiled. "That's good to know." I smiled at him and Ginger turned her wrath on him. "What kind of man are you to allow her to be in another man's house and God only knows what they were doing."

"You're correct about one fact I am a man so that means I trust and respect my wife you on the other hand caused this man to fall into a drunken stupor after he found out you were pregnant." Julian stood behind me and I felt like I had lost the ability to breathe. "So you cause this man to become sick and call my wife a bitch."

Ginger screamed, "You're trying to hurt us because your wife is in love with my man."

"Well I told Alonzo to get a DNA test as soon as possible." Julian laughed and Ginger ran out the door crying.

Julian looked at me when he heard me cough. "Alisha baby are you okay?"

"Yes Julian but is that true?"

"Is what true?"

"Is Ginger pregnant?" I said slowly

"Yeah he told us yesterday on the golf course and was puzzle as to how it happened." Julian laughed aloud "I told him it's when you stick your di...sorry baby."

I mumbled, "He said that he never did."

"Yeah that's what he sai...wait how did you know?"

"Julian we talk so I know."

"No why the hell are you talking to him about that."

"Julian calm down."

"No Alisha you're going to answer me."

"I can't its private."

"I'm your husband."

"It's not what you think but something happened to him years ago and he thought, I can't tell you but was before we were together."

"We will talk about this later."

"Hey what's going on Alisha's tires have been slashed?" Tommy asked as he strolled in.

Julian ran to the door. "That psycho bitch." He pulled out his phone and called a tow company. Here take my keys so you can drive my car home and we will take care of Alonzo."

"Don't let him lay on his back he might aspirate."

"If you don't get your non MD butt out of here I know that." Julian shouted. I walked to the car and went home

Julian and Tommy rolled him over on his stomach before sitting down to watch TV. A few hours later Julian said, "Thomas I think Alisha is still in love with this dude."

"Well you know y'all got married the same week they broke up and he asked her to marry him." Julian looked at Tommy. "Hell no, I didn't realize that." Julian stood up. "Man Alisha tells me everything but when it comes to him I don't know any details."

"Julian that man broke her heart but you were the one she gave up everything for."

"Thomas was I just a rebound and she needed to find love or did I really make her heart leap?"

"You made her heart leap." Alonzo said sitting up. "Julian if you were not the man for Alisha she would have never married you."

"He's right" Tommy chimed in.

"How do you know?" Julian asked.

"Because, you were not the first man that ask her to get married that week."

Tommy chimed in, "That month or year."

"Men fall in love with your wife but she's real picky and stubborn." Alonzo said.

"I know that but I tricked her and surprised her with a wedding."

"It doesn't matter she would have said no if she had doubts or you were not the one." Tommy blurted out.

Alonzo stood up trying to straighten himself up, "Julian your wife will never cheat on you and I would not disrespect our friendship by being with her but yes I will always love your wife; didn't you?"

"Yes every day I was with Rasheda I thought about something that damn woman did." Julian was thinking about our past. "That woman brought me a joy I can't explain and I've never had that with another woman."

"Yes just be glad because she's brought a wrath that was unforgettable when a man upset her as well." Tommy said shaking his head as he shivered. "How can something that tiny and sweet be so mean?"

"Thank God I've never seen it." Alonzo said

"That's good because I came close and that was enough." Julian said thinking back.

Julian stood up and patted Alonzo on the back as he raised his glass to Tommy. "If I would've died in that plane crash Alonzo I would rest in peace knowing you were with my widow or you Thomas if you were not with Isabella."

"Ok it's time to stop drinking Julian." Tommy laughed

"No man I'm serious if I were to die tomorrow I want Alisha to be with a man who will love her the way she should be loved and you two guys have been great friends to my wife, my children , and me. She deserves the best and if I can't be there second best would be you guys." Julian roared with laughter.

"Ok Julian that's where you were going," Tommy said waving his arms letting Julian know he was number one.

Isabella and I had dinner together because I knew the men were going to be out for a while. I called Julian around 10:30 to check on them but the call went to voice mail so I called back. I could hear laughter in the background before he responded, "Hey baby, I'm sorry I didn't call we were reminiscing." I heard Tommy explode into laughter.

"I just wanted to check on you guys before I went to bed alone."

Julian's demeanor and voice changed, "So, you need me to come home?"

Tommy yelled, "Why are you whispering Julian?"

"Shut up Thomas my wife needs me."

Tommy and Alonzo kept giving Julian a hard time as we talked. "Baby I'll see you tomorrow have fun with the guys."

"Love you." We hung up and they continued to laugh at him."

Julian turned the tables on Alonzo. "Wait man, how can you laugh your phone has gone off so many times you cut it off now who was that?" Julian put his hand up to his ear. "I can't hear you...what now." Alonzo stood up as they laughed at him.

Julian came home early the next morning and pleased me before he went to play golf.

Truth

A few months later in the wee hours of the morning while I was soothing Lil J downstairs so I wouldn't wake Julian and Millie. I was startled by someone banging on the door. Julian came running down stairs with his gun. "Alisha where are you?" He whispered.

"I'm in here Julian." I whispered from the doorway. Julian cocked his gun and yelled, "Who is it?"

"It's me Tommy Ma Carrie passed out."

"Alisha, get in her." Julian yelled as he snatched open the door. "Thomas did you call 911?"

"Yes, Isabella is up there with her but I had to get Alisha." He said in a panic.

Julian grabbed Lil J and exclaimed, "Get some clothes on and go!" Just then an ambulance roared up the street and Tommy took off. Within seconds I was running down the stairs. Julian yelled as he handed me the keys. "Drive up so you can follow them to the hospital." I jumped in the car

and met Tommy at the door as they carried
her out. When followed in my car, "Have
you called your parents Tommy?" I said as I
followed the ambulance to the hospital. He
pulled out his phone and called his parents
and Marcus but had to leave a message
because no one answered. I dropped
Tommy off at the ER entrance and parked.

When I walked into the ER and saw
George Oscuro sitting in the corner he
looked as if he had been crying. I walked
over to him. "Hi George it's me Dr. Alisha
Carothers are you alright?"
He looked up and tears fell from his eyes.
"It's my fourteen year old daughter OD on
drugs and they are trying to get her
stabilized."
I sat next to him to comfort him saying, "I'm
sure the Doctors..."
"It's your fault I should've kept her away
from you." The woman screamed as a man
was pulling her back. The man tried to
calm her but she continued to cry
uncontrollably. Tanisha was the woman
and she is the mother of Tiffney of their
fourteen year old.

Tanisha lied about her age after running
away from home and married George two
years later. After she turned twenty she
divorced George went back to school and

gave up her party girl life style. I later found out the man, Derek, was her husband.

"Is this one of your new bitches?" she barked.

"No." George said, "She's my Therapist."

"Are you fucking him too like the last two?" she asked rolling her eyes.

George blurted out, "No she's not she has class you hatful bitch." I stood up and stepped back as they continued to argue. "It was his brother that drugged up our daughter while he fucked her in that hotel room where I found her." He became enraged as he spoke and walked out after saying something I couldn't comprehend.

I eased over to the ER check in to ask about Ma Carrie when my phone rang.

"Hello."

"Alisha its Tommy they have her stabilized and she wants to see you so the nurse is coming to get you." He whispered and hung up. A nurse walked out and called my name to escort me to the room. "Hey Ma Carrie, how are you feeling?" I said as I walked in "I'm feeling much better having both of you here." She said smiling as a tear rolled down her cheek. "Come closer so I can talk to both of you." Tommy and I stood as close to her bedside as possible before she put our hands together. "I've watched you two grow, fall in love and bear fruit but it brings me joy to know you will always love and be a part of each other's life." She took a deep breath as more tears fell. "I always thought you would be together forever and you will just not the way we hoped but the friendship you share is more than we could've asked for." Ma Carrie tried to sit up but Tommy stopped her. "Tommy my will is in the bottom draw of that beautiful chest you bought me." As she took a deep breath Tommy started to speak. "Hush up Tommy now y'all take care of each other because I love you." She smiled took a breath and closed her eyes. Tommy screamed and fell to his knees. The nurses ran in to assist her as I tried to pull him out of the way.

Ma Carrie was put on life support but left instructions in her will to take her off after seventy-two hours. The family came up and prayed over her but Tommy and I knew Ma Carrie was ready to go. She passed on a month after they removed her from life-support. Tommy's mother and father blamed him for her health condition because he wanted to be around me and bringing her here was too much on her. Those accusations turned into a big fight so Tommy's parents and sister's went to a hotel for the rest of their stay. When the other family members came up they stayed in my old house. The will was read the day after she was passed because her body had to be readied and shipped back home for burial.

The will was read at Tommy's house and his parents tried to fight that arrangement because they were upset but Ma Carrie requested it. The family arrived around one thirty for a light meal so the reading started at two o'clock on the dot. Tommy's mother and sisters rolled their eyes at Isabella and me for different reasons. The lawyer started with a short speech Ma Carrie wanted him to read. "Mrs. Brown wanted to me to read this document first before reading the will ending with a short video." He said rambling through his briefcase pulling out a CD before he continued. "Carrie Louise Brown being of sound mind stated the following..." After reading the short statement her will revealed that she only left money to the children under eighteen. The house to Tommy's father and her jewelry was given to me except her wedding rings which were given to Tommy for his son Thomas. The biggest surprise was the money she left Marcus to jump start his new life. After the reading of the will which caused eye rolling, folded arms, and turned up faces the Lawyer started the CD in which Ma Carrie stated facts she would not leave untold. "First I would like to state Tommy was conceived out of wedlock yes you heard me so Christian you and that fake stuck-up wife of yours my daughter can get off your high horse and treat people right." She said smacking her lips as she sat up. "Tommy your daddy was a rolling stone and that's why he wanted you to marry that bitch Lisa her brother was your daddy's son." She sat back and the gasping in the room could be heard a mile away but I smiled because I knew most of the secrets. When I was little I would sit on the stairs and listen to Ma Carrie and Grams talking in the parlor or they would try to talk over my head while they were sittin a spell with each other. Ma Carrie was not done she told one more big secret before she ended the video. As she sat back in the big chair looking directly into the camera folding her arms you could see her anger all over her face. "Lisa was the one that set up Alisha to be raped that summer." She twisted her lips. "The sheriff's sons, his brothers sons, the mayor's son, Jessie Mae's granddaughter, and Mother Bell's great granddaughter was in it." Ma Carrie's eyes filled with tears. "I'm glad Jessie Mae's granddaughter went crazy and Mother Bell's grandson moved away taking that evil heifer with him." She wiped her eyes before she continued. "Tommy and Alisha should've been a couple but that caused a hurt in Alisha that wasn't eased until she had Millie and was revealed to her after she married Julian." Ma Carrie smiled and sat up. "Alisha followed my advice and I'm going to say it to my desperate granddaughters." She adjusted herself so she could point her finger. "A man that findth a wife, which means you've already been equipped to be a wife not preparing to be one. He finds a good thing that is why it is not the other way around because if he's good he will find you and find favor with God. I said this to let you women know to keep your legs closed until your wedding night and then you have no need to wonder what you are to him because you've set standards. Neither one of you will long for someone else because your spouse will be the only one you know. Women don't respect themselves anymore but have the nerve to want someone to respect them." Ma Carrie laughed and sat back in the chair before ending with this last statement. "Men stop playing with these women if you want her and respect her wait until you get married but if all you want to do is play with her let her know up front and stop playing with her emotions by letting her make a choice to be a lay-up or stand-up woman. I love you all now put aside the past and love each other." Ma Carrie waved as the CD cut off.

Some sat in shock, others had tears or smiles, but Tommy's father stormed out as Tommy and his mother ran after him. He sat in the car crying as he gripped the steering wheel until his knuckles turned white. "Christian, unlock the door so I can get in." Tommy's mother exclaimed. He looked at her and slowly reached over to unlock the door. Tommy jumped in and for the next two hours they sat in the car. Other family members received instruction and paperwork before they left to return home. After the house cleared Ms. Daniels and Julian took the kids to our house while Isabella and I cleaned up. Isabella kept running to the window to check on Tommy. "Isabella what are you worried about?" I asked.
"I don't want them to hurt my Thomas." She said nervously.
"Don't worry they won't?" I laughed
She sat on the sofa and gave a heavy sigh before saying, "They've never accepted me and my family hates him."

I sat down next to her and put my arm around her. "It has nothing to do with you but it was their own demons they were dealing with."

She looked up at me and smiled, "You're right Alisha because Ma Carrie would always say the same thing." We got up and continued putting up the chairs when Tommy and his parents walked in. "Alisha can we be alone for a few moments." Tommy said so I started towards the door when Tommy's father grabbed my hand and squeezed it without saying a word I saw the apology in his eyes so I returned his jester with a smile and silently walked out the door. When I got home I hugged my husband and babies.

The next day Tommy called, "Alisha you'll never guess what happened."

"You're right Tommy I won't so tell me." I said full of annoyance. I hated the guess what game and he knew it.

"My parents are staying for a few more days." Tommy said it so fast and with such excitement I thought I heard him wrong.

"Say that again Tommy?"

He calmed down and repeated his statement. "My parents are staying longer than planned so that they can start building a relationship with my family."

I was in shock but excited for Tommy.
"That's great Tommy."
"Now Alisha this is where I need your help."
Tommy said with caution.
"You know I'll do anything within reason for
you Tommy."
"Good, will you and Julian have dinner with
us tonight?"
I took a deep breath so my words would
flow out with joy. "Yes Tommy we would be
glad to."
"Great." He announced "I'll see you tonight.

Julian walked into the bedroom with a
sleeping Lil J and asked, "What's wrong
with you babe?"
I smiled as I stood up to meet them.
"Tommy wants us to have dinner with his
parents."
"Hell no!" Julian exclaimed.
I was stunned so I grabbed the baby when
he jumped and asked, "Why not"
"Those bastards knew who raped you and
protected them." Julian grabbed the baby
and put him in his playpen before ushering
me into the sitting area within our
bedroom. "Look Alisha I can take a lot of
stuff but they hurt you and I remember
how they treated you." He kissed my
forehead as he embraced me.
"Julian I understand but I'm doing this for

Tommy because I love him." I said caressing his tighten cheek.

Julian eased to his knees in front of me and said, "I love Thomas as well but because I'm in love with my beautiful wife I'll do it." We smiled at each other and started kissing which was leading into more when Millie said, "DJ why are you holding mama down to kiss her?"

He jumped up and covered his rising excitement with a pillow from our little girl. Julian yelled, "Millie what are you doing in here didn't I tell you if the door is closed not to enter this room?" I started smiling because the door wasn't closed and I knew he was embarrassed. Millie cried, "DJ the door was open and I wanted to play with my brother." I burst into laughter and tears ran down my face because Julian always feared Millie walking in on us. "Shut-up Alisha it's not that funny." He barked. Millie's eyes widened and covered her mouth as she said "DJ said a bad word." Julian was undone and picked up Millie. "I'm sorry baby."

"No, to mommy." She commanded pointing to me.

Julian turned to me and kissed me on the forehead. "I'm sorry baby."

"Good now let's go." Millie said jumping down and running out the door.

Julian turned towards me and said, "Let's have another baby."

I looked at him a little puzzled, "Where did that come from?"

He pulled me closer and wrapped his arms around me, "I love you and everything that comes from you and I just feel like we need to have another child before it's too late."

"Julian we can start as soon as you lock the door." I said smiling as I pulled my dress up so Julian ran to the door. When he came back to the sofa and started to caress me with his tongue the baby screamed out.

"Damn." Julian said falling out on the floor so I got up to see about the baby. "Take him to Ms. Daniels so we can finish." Julian moaned through his hands that covered his face.

"No you do it Mr. Want more kids." I laughed.

He got up and rushed over to me and wrapped his arms around me after I took Junior out of the playpen. "I love you so much Alisha it seems as if I'm dreaming."

"That's not going to work Julian." I said turning towards him "But I will give you a quickie in about five minutes."

Julian smiled and I picked up Lil J.

We walked down stairs. "It's about time." Ms. Daniels said.

"For what Ms. Daniels," I asked looking puzzled.

"Their walk, now put that boy down he can walk." She winked at me and smiled. I knew then what she was doing so I handed her lil Julian and grabbed Julian's hand as I ran back up stairs. "We'll be gone for at least an hour." She yelled at our backs.

Julian and I experienced freedom in the bedroom for the first during the day since we moved into our new home. When we got upstairs he was ripping off clothes in the corridor so he was undressed before we made it to the bedroom. "Julian don't you want to go into the strip club?" I asked "No take off your clothes and get ready to scream your head off." He said as he open the skylights to let in more light. I did as he commanded and for the next hour I enjoyed my husband like never before. As I lay on my comatose husband's chest his phone rang so I got up to answer it. "Hello."

"Bitch what are you doing answering my man's phone." She barked.

"Rasheda" I responded calmly.

"Yes it's me you man stealing slut so put my husband on the phone." She sneered

"He's sleep so you need to call back." I said holding back my annoyance.

"You're a liar put him on the phone." She

yelled

"He's asleep but I will tell him you called good bye." I said hanging up the phone but she called right back so I blocked her calls. I lay on my husband's chest and we slept for the next forty-five minutes.

I awoke and got in the shower within two minutes Julian had eased into the shower with me and we started the pleasure again but this time we went deeper with the pleasure. By the time we got out of the shower we were exhausted again but clean so we got dressed and went down stairs for a late lunch. Ms. Daniels chuckled, "I see you've rekindled that lost fire from the old house."

"Yes Ms. Daniels we have and I think we've found some." I laughed "Thank you."

"I was young and married once so I know life can have a toll on a relationship." She sighed and stared into the room as if she could see her life before speaking again. "You are blessed because you both have more than love for each other. When I see the two of you I see admiration, respect, and you adore each other. Most people believe being in love is all you need but loving a person fades during augments, mounting bill, and hunger pains. Then there are the children and a lack of desire because of life so, the grass is greener on the other side syndrome hits and now you're cheating on your mate. This comes because everything is nurtured except your relationship with your partner."

Julian looked at me and smiled. "Yes I'm truly blessed." He looked at Ms. Daniels, "If we wanted more kids would you be alright with that?"

"Have as many as you can, I gave birth to ten but lost two in delivery, three before they were five, two before the age of eighteen, two as adults and the one living won't speak to me." Ms. Daniels eyes begun to water and she gave a sigh. "Well I think it's time for the four of you to plan a trip to some exotic place and get your fire back."

"The four of us," I said puzzled.

"Yes child the two couples with no children on their vacation." She said as she walked out pointing towards Tommy house.

Two hours had passed during our conversation of teaching and revelation. The kids didn't wake up until Ms. Daniels went to her room. Julian and I played with Millie and Junior until Tommy called. "Alisha we're leaving at seven would y'all like to ride or drive?"

"Hold on Tommy let me ask Julian." I turned and asked Julian. I told Tommy

what Julian said, "He wanted to know if you wanted a limo so we can all drink."
Tommy panicked "No no we can't drink."
I laughed, "Tommy it was a joke."
"Tell Julian we can't play like that with them it's too important." He hung up without a response.

A few hours Tommy, Isabella, Cole, and his parents were at the door. Julian was still upstairs getting ready. Ms. Daniels answered the door. "Hello Ponder family."
"Hello Ms. Daniels." they said as she picked Cole up and took him into the house. "I'm ready." Julian announced as he came down the stairs. "How is everyone this evening?" Everyone seemed to be uncomfortable so we walked to the car and drove to the restaurant in silence except for Julian and I.

When we arrived at the restaurant as usual George met us at the door and gave us the royal treatment. We were seated and ordered drinks. Julian ordered the appetizers. Tommy's father leaned over and whispered, "These prices are ridicules let's go somewhere else."
"Dad that's fine I can afford it." Tommy smiled.
"It's not what you can afford but about being a good steward of that which God has

blessed you with." He grumbled and Tommy's chest sank. Tommy looked sick and Isabella looked scared as her eyes pleaded with me for help. I whispered to Julian and he kissed my hand. "There is a time and place for everything and that was uncalled for but you are your mother's daughter." Christian uttered.

"Man I don't care who you are or how you treat your son but my wife and family you will not disrespect." Julian quickly retorted. Tommy looked as if was about to have a heart attack but Isabella smiled. "I will not stand for this disrespectful heathen talking to me in such a manner I'm a Bishop." He said standing up.

"If you don't sit your self-righteous pompous ass down" Julian said as he stood up and leaned across the table. "You are not God but an overseer that should humble yourself to those you serve not the other way around." He stood up right. "That's my problem with church they put people like you and Pastors on a pedestal and you are just as or even more so as imperfect as we are and that is why God called you because of that everlasting thorn or sinful desire in your heart that is supposed to humble you not cause you to be superior."

Tommy was hyperventilating by this time so

Isabella started to panic as I sat back and smiled. Tommy's father sat down and his mother was as pale as a ghost. Tommy became angry but the waitress walked up before he could speak. Julian ordered for everyone and the table was silent as everyone stared at their plates except a fleeting glance here and there between Tommy and me. Julian paid and the ride home was uncomfortably silent. Julian dropped them off at home and Tommy never said a word he just stormed out the car but Isabella said good bye.

Ten minutes after we walked into the house Tommy was at the door. "Hey Tommy I'm glad you came by."
"I came to get my son."
"But he's sleep."
"Should I call the authorities to remove my son from your home?" he said abruptly.
"No come in I'll get him."
Julian walked up. "Babe, why did you leave the door open?"
He looked outside. "Hey Thomas come on in."
Tommy never acknowledged him and turned his back. Julian hunched his shoulders and walked into the house. I brought Cole down stairs and gave him to Tommy and he walked away without saying

a word. I walked back into the house and called Isabella. "I can't talk to you anymore Alisha." She whispered.

"Why?"

"Because Thomas is mad at your husband and you didn't stop him."

"Well I'll be here if you need me I love you guys."

"Bye Alisha he's walking in now." She quickly hung up.

I ran upstairs and told Julian. "Babe I'm sorry Thomas is upset with you but like I said I don't like those people."

"I know but I miss him already."

"If he's your friend he'll be back just let him cool off."

"You're right Julian." I said as I snuggled up next to him.

The silence ended after Tommy had gone home for two weeks and was sitting in my living room with some flowers. "Alisha I'm sorry." He hugged me "Will you forgive me."

I smiled and screamed, "Yes"

Julian came running down stairs. "Are you ready to go man?"

"Yeah, the guys are meeting us there."

"Wait what's going on."

"I told Thomas we couldn't play golf until he apologized to you."

"Both of y'all suck." I said throwing the

flowers down.
I went into the kitchen to cook for the kids and they ran out the door laughing.

That evening after they played golf the guys; Julian, Tommy, Alonzo, Mr. Avery and Mike came to our house for dinner. Isabella, Donna, Ms. Daniels, and I set up for our first family dinner. Mrs. Avery and Ginger were not invited because they were too messy besides that Mr. Avery and Alonzo didn't want them there. This was perfect because holidays were hectic. When the guys came in we set the table. Before we ate I noticed that Ms. Daniels was a little giggly sitting next to Mr. Avery. After dinner we sat around talking but Mike had too much and passed out on the sofa. Ms. Daniels and Mr. Avery retired to the front porch with coffee.

In the morning we made a head count of everyone who stayed over and prepared breakfast.

Confusion

Julian and I started to fool around when his phone started ringing. "Hello" he answered the phone I slid between his legs. "George what's go... shit?" "Your what?" Julian said standing up pushing me away. Julian hung up, "Baby George's daughter is in the hospital again and he got arrested for beating the guy that gave her the drugs." He said trying to think. I was wondering why George called him instead of someone else and how did he know Julian's number by heart. "I need you to go to the hospital while I go bail George out" he said making another phone call. I put my clothes back on and went to tell Ms. Daniels where I was going when Julian shot out the door like a rocket. I drove to the hospital pondering questions about what just happened tonight.

When I got to the hospital I saw Tanisha sitting in the corner by herself crying. "Tanisha are you alright?" I asked as I sat down next to her. She looked up at me as if she had given up. "My baby is on life support and I can't do a thing." She wiped her eyes. "Her father is in jail for beating the guy that was in the room with her which was my husband." Tears started to flow again. "Where did I go wrong she was my only child?"

"Well I'm going to sit with you until George gets here." I said rubbing her back. I guess it took her a moment to comprehend what I had said. "Wait are you one of George's girl friends?" she said moving away from me. "No he called my husband so my husband went to bail him out."

"So why are you here?"

"Because my husband told me to come sit with you until they arrived." Julian had connections with everyone so by the time he got there George was being released. We sat and talked for what seemed like hours when George came running over to Tanisha. "Tanisha is she alright?"

She started crying again. "I don't know George they won't let me go back after she crashed the second time."

"We will stay here with you until you find out something." Julian volunteered.

"Thanks Julian and Dr. Carothers."

Tanisha looked up and saw Derek's brother walk in with his son so she jumped up and ran over to them. "What the hell are you doing here?" she screamed. Before they could say anything George picked her up and carried her outside until she calmed down. When George and Tanisha had come back in they were already in the back. They had brought her husband Derek here after George finished beating him. When they came from the back I spotted Derek and whispered to Julian to get George's attention so he wouldn't see him but it was too late Tanisha had already seen Derek and was quickly walking over to him. She was yelling so loud security came running out before George could reach her. Derek ran out because he knew he had been sleeping with a minor and didn't want to go to jail. The guard released her after she calmed down and George picked her up. Five minutes later the Doctor came out and I knew what was about to happen so I whispered it to Julian. Tanisha fell to her knees and George picked her up and motioned with his head for Julian's assistance. They put her in a chair while George went to the back to see his daughter. I walked over to Julian and hugged him. George came out twenty minutes later and asked if we could take them home. Julian took them home while I went back home. I told Julian that it didn't

feel right and we should call a cab or car service but Julian felt as if he had to. We kissed and I told Julian I loved him and he reassured me that everything was going to be alright. "Alisha you mean the world to me and we have a family that I would never do anything to jeopardize." He pulled me closer. "Alisha if I thought this was dangerous for a second I would not take them home I have too much to lose." He kissed my stomach and then my forehead before he closed the door. "I'll keep you on the phone until I get home."
I smiled and said, "Thanks babe." I drove him to his car and he called two minutes later.

I was almost home before they had even left the Hospital. When I pulled up Tommy was on the porch. "Hold on Julian Tommy's here."
"Tell him to go home." Julian laughed.
"Hey Tommy, what's up?"
"I tried to call Julian and he never answered so I called you and both cars were gone." He said looking uneasy
"Is everything okay?" I asked becoming worried.
"Isabella's having twins and I'm scared."
"Why?"
"I don't know" Tommy looked at the moon

as we talked. Isabella looked as if she was about to give birth any day now but I knew Tommy and something else was wrong.

"Be honest Tommy, what's really bothering you?"

"Isabella wanted to reach out to her family since I became close to my parents so they will be here next month."

"That's great."

"No its not they want to bring her brothers and the guy she was going to marry and they want to stay in our house."

"That's not so good."

"So have you talked to her about it?"

"Yes and she wants them to stay with us."

"The ex- boyfriend too?"

"Yes because like us Alisha they were childhood friends."

"Well I will be there for you and if anything jumps off; I am sure Julian will have your back."

"I know."

"Wait Tommy I heard something."

"Julian, Julian oh my God Julian baby answer me."

"What's wrong?" Tommy exclaimed.

"I heard gun shots and screams." I shouted so I cut the tracking device on to find his phone and jumped in my car. Tommy pulled me out and yelled, "Call 911 and let me drive." I started calling and I told the police George's name, what I heard, and Julian's tag number. We drove and I kept talking into the earpiece because I knew Julian could hear me if he was alive. I heard a moan and screamed, "Julian is that you baby?" I listen for a few seconds and shouted, "Tommy what am I going to do?"

"Alisha calm down…"

I yelled "I hear siren and somebody is talking to Julian." Someone said we have a pulse. I screamed again, "Tommy he's alive." I shook Tommy and someone picked up the phone, "Hello."

"This is the driver's wife, what hospital should we go to?"

"Ma'am I'm going to let you talk to an officer." He handed the phone to an officer. "Whom am I speaking with?"

"This is Dr. Alisha Carothers and my husband Julian Carothers is the driver of the black SUV tag MODEL1.1."

The officer asked, "Does your husband deal in illegal narcotics?"

"No my husband is a retired CFO of a major company and he's rich."

"Ma'am that does not mean he's not selling drugs."

I realized I had to put on my professional attitude with this dude. "You are correct officer…" I continued until he told me the hospital they were going to. I called his parents to let them know everything and they called a friend.

When we got there I asked for him and was ushered to a waiting room. "Hi mom and dad have you heard anything?"
"Yes he's still in surgery"
"Alisha what was he doing there?" His father asked puzzled.
"The owner of the house is the same guy from the flying school..." When I finished telling the story Julian's father became enraged and walked out. Five hours later the Doctor came out and told us we could see him as soon as he was in recovery.

George was on life support awaiting his family to make a decision and Tanisha was killed instantly. Tommy came back and his eyes were red. "Are you alright Alisha?"
"Yes Tommy but I'm scared." I said reaching for his hand. Julian's mother had been sedated and was in a room. The nurse that accompanied the doctor earlier reappeared and took us to his room. I text the room number to his father and took a deep breath before I entered. When I walked in my mind flashed back to Grams and Papa when they were in the hospital. So tears formed in my eyes but I was determined to be strong for my husband. The closer I got

the weaker I became. "Can you do this Alisha?" Tommy said holding my arm as tears rolled down his face. "Yes I have to touch him. When I reached him I couldn't see through the tears that flowed uncontrollably down my face. "Julian baby I love you." I said as I reached for his hand and squeezed it. Tears formed in Tommy's eyes as we looked at my husband. "Tommy I can't leave him." I said as I lay on his chest. "I'll take care of the kids don't worry and I'll bring you food or whatever else you need." Tommy kissed me on m forehead and walked out because he couldn't be strong.

When Tommy got to my house Ms. Daniels was waiting at the door. "How is he Thomas?" She yelled
"He's out of surgery but it doesn't look good." He muttered. "I need to pack some clothes and stuff for Lisha and take them to her in the morning." She helped him pack a bag and he took what seemed like the longest walk home. He walked in to a crying Isabella. "It's in God's hands so everything is going to be alright." He said reassuring her.

The next morning Julian opened his eyes and called out, "Alisha." I jumped up and rushed over to my husband. "Julian baby you're alive." I joyfully squealed.

"Baby I'm sorry I'll never do that again."

"Julian you didn't do anything you were shot."

"What how...who?"

"It's a long story don't worry about it." I said patting him on the hand and smiling. A Detective walked in and walked up to Julian. "Hello Mr. Carothers I'm Detective Jones and I want to talk to you about last night."

"Okay but I don't remember anything."

"You are a lucky man because your companions are dead so we really need your help."

Julian looked puzzled. "Companion, what companions?"

"The people you were with last night George and Tanisha."

"I know George we went to flight school together and my wife was his counselor." The detective turned around to look at me.

"So you represented him in his drug convictions?" He smirked.

"No his Psychiatrist," I gave a fake halfhearted smiled.

"Well excuse me." He said swing his hips and arms.

"The victims were at the hospital because George found his daughter at a hotel; she overdosed and died so my husband took them home."

"Really so why did your husband bail him out of jail?"

I rolled my eyes at him because I realized he was just stupid. "He was arrested for beating the man who gave his minor daughter the drugs which was her step-father."

"Really..."

"Officer how may I help you?" Julian's father bellowed.

"It's detective and I'm investigating this drug dealer." He replied smugly.

"Well Officer I suggest you come back at a later time and my son is no drug dealer." His dad called the Mayor.

"Look you don't tell me what to do." The detective's phone rung, "Hello Yes sir yes sir." He hung up and said "This isn't over." He said walking out.

"Yes it is." Julian's father said sternly. As the officer stormed out of the room.

"Hello dad," I said smiling.

"Hello Alisha honey, how's he doing?"

"He opened his eyes but couldn't remember what happened."

"Is he still awake?"

"No sir."

"Now tell me what's going on." His father said holding my hand.

"I told you everything last night."

"I had someone check those people out and that woman's husband is a drug dealer."

"He was." I said surprised

"Yes, you didn't know."

"No and I don't think she did either well maybe that's why George beat him."

"Well that might be true" He paused and walked towards his son taking a deep breath before he walked out. I walked to the bedside to hold my husband's hand. I leaned onto his chest and fell asleep. Tommy walked in and woke me up. "Hey Lisha how are you?"

I smiled, "Hi Tommy thanks for coming."

He walked closer "I brought you some food and clothes." Tommy had fear across his face.

"Are you alright Tommy?"

"Yes I'm just scared."

"That's understandable Tommy."

"Was Julian into any illegal activity?"

"No why?"

"A Detective came by and asked Ms. Daniels some question but a lawyer came over and told him he had to leave."

"He wasn't but Derek was." I sighed

"George was trying to protect his daughter and now all of these lives lost over a high." Julian called out again and I ran to his side. "Yes Julian"

"I love you."

"I love you too." He was trying to get up.

"Julian what are you doing?"

"I'm trying to see you and the baby is he alright?"

"Yes she's fine." I waved Tommy over. "Tommy's here."

"Hey Julian can't wait to beat you on the course."

Julian smiled "Only if I'm still in here." They laughed.

We talked for a while.

"Thomas did you know we were..." Julian started coughing and his machines started going off. I knew he was going to be alright so I stepped back to let the nurse work. A nurse ran in and hit the call button for a help because Julian was crashing. I kept saying, "I know everything was going to be alright." I walked into the hall with Tommy. Fifteen minutes later the Doctor came out and gave me the news. My husband was gone and my reaction never changed because I knew he was going to be alright. Tommy took me home and I went upstairs and fell asleep.

Tommy came over that evening to check on me but I was still asleep. He walked down stairs, "Ms. Daniels has she been up?"

"No Thomas she hasn't made a peep or come out of that room." She was wringing her hands and pacing. "Go check her again and make sure she's breathing." Ms. Daniels said looking up towards my bed room.

"She's alive and Tommy stay out of my room." I laughed.

"Lisha are you alright?"

"Yes, I have to be for my children and the last minute arrangements."

"Alisha, you need to let his lawyer and us worry about that." Ms. Daniels commanded.

"Yeah Lisha" Tommy chimed in.

I reached for my ringing cell phone. It was Julian's father. "Alisha I just wanted you to know that George guy was legit and so was Tanisha but her husband wasn't and he knew Rasheda."

After hearing her name I remembered her threats but I'm sure she didn't because this was an accident. "Alisha I have someone looking into the matter."

I went back upstairs and cried. Tommy came in and asked, "What happen?"

"Rasheda knew the husband Derek."

"What does that mean?"

"It may not have been an accident."

"Oh my God, Lisha" Tommy stood up. "I'm

going to get you something to eat because you have to keep up your strength." He rushed out so I turned over and went to sleep. When Tommy came back I made him sit the food down and leave so I could rest. I stayed in my room until the funeral.

At the funeral Rasheda was escorted out because of her antics. His father was still investigating her. The gunmen had been arrested and my husband's death was on the front page because it was big news. Everyone was calling so Ms. Daniels stopped answering the home phone and we went to the old house for some peace until the reading of the will. Donna was not taking his death well and had to be hospitalized so she couldn't make the funeral. The reading of the will was an even bigger circus because of Rasheda. Her children had a college fund and received money at eighteen, twenty-one, and twenty-five. She wanted money now but he bought a small house for them and she was the overseer until they were of age. Our children had a trust set up but they could start receiving funds at sixteen. He even had a trust fund for our unborn child that we had not revealed to anyone yet. Rasheda didn't think it was fair because Millie was not his daughter, he never claimed Julian II, and the unborn child was not his. She was removed again and her kids cried.

After the funeral and reading of the will I went back to my room and stayed there for a few days. Tommy, Ms. Daniels, and Isabella tried to get me out the room but nothing worked. That Friday Alonzo came over to pick up the kids knocked on my bed room door. He slowly opened it and called out, "Alisha, damn this is nice." He said walking down the corridor that led to the master bedroom. "Alisha, are you decent?" He walked into the room as I walked out of the bathroom and looked down because my robe was open. "Alonzo what are you doing here?" I exclaimed closing my robe.
"Baby I came to check on you." He said as he turned around. "Please put on some clothes."
I picked up some sweats and a tee shirt before I walked over to him. "Alonzo I'm dressed."
"Alisha, how are you?" His eyes were searching for the truth in my face.
I flopped down on the bed and sighed, "Alonzo it's so hard." Alonzo came and sat next to me on the bed and put his arms around me. "Alisha I'm here if you need me." Alonzo held me and kissed me on the

forehead as I cried. Before I knew it he was kissing me. I quickly pulled back and Alonzo jumped up in a panic "Oh my god I'm sorry Alisha."

I cried harder and fell back on the bed as Alonzo ran out of the room.

I came down stairs an hour later but the children were gone and Tommy was asleep on the sofa. "Ms. Daniels is there anything to eat."

"Oh child you're a sight for sore eyes." She hugged and kissed on me until I asked again. "I'm sorry Alisha." She ran into the kitchen. "So how's the baby?"

"I have an appointment Monday."

"Good."

"Hey Alisha I'm glad you're up." Tommy hugged me from behind and rubbed my belly, "How are you feeling?"

"I'm good Tommy." We walked into the living room. Ms. Daniels brought me my food and we talked until the wee hours of the morning. Isabella had curled up on the sofa and went to sleep, Ms. Daniels took the recliner, and Tommy and I sat on the floor talking about everything in our life.

On Monday Alonzo took me to the doctor. After my check-up I rushed through the waiting room and out the door. Alonzo had to run to catch up with me. "Alisha, are you alright?"

"Yes I just need to go home and see the kids."

"Alisha is the baby okay?"

"Alonzo just take me home."

When we got there I ran in and held Millie and Julian as they ran up to me.

"Alisha it's going to be alright." Ms. Daniels said.

"What wrong." Alonzo whispered to Ms. Daniels.

"Lil. J's birthday is today and his party is this weekend."

"I thought something was wrong with the baby."

"Call Thomas and let him know." Mr. Avery advised

"Yes sir."

That week both children sleep with me. Tommy and Alonzo went on with the party as planned. Mr. Avery was there along with Mike and Rasheda kids; Donna couldn't make it.

Imperfection

Mr. Avery spent more time at our house after he moved in with Alonzo because Ginger and Mrs. Avery were driving him crazy. He chose his room which was downstairs next to Ms. Daniels. They became tag team babysitters for all of us. Donna was not able to spend time with her grandchildren after Julian's death so Rasheda kids spent more time with Mike and us. Three months before Julian's death they practically lived with his parents. They were already spending a lot of time with us anyway so we had already given them bedrooms at our house when Julian first bought it but Rasheda would not let them come over. Rasheda had been MIA for a while so she just dropped off the kids with Mike and left so he hired a full time nanny.

Tommy's in-laws would be there in three days and he was in panic mode so Mr. Avery and Alonzo took him to play golf every day to ease his mind. I sat with Isabella for a couple of days before returning to work. I really wanted to avoid the house because all I could think about was Julian.

The day finally arrived and Tommy sent a car to pick up his in-laws. They were there around twelve so Tommy set up a big picnic in the back so we could all meet and greet each other. When Isabella's father saw the house he was amazed and her mother was shocked. They greeted her and we retired to the back. Everyone got along and the family accepted Tommy. It was as if we had known each other for years so by night fall everyone was still there. Around eight we went into the house. Ms. Daniels and Mr. Avery took the kids to my house and got them ready for bed. By midnight everyone over fifty had retired for the night and I was ready to go but Alonzo kept asking me to stay. We finally made our departure twenty minutes later but the others were still talking.

Alonzo walked me home so we sat in my backyard for a while talking and looking at the moon. "I love this swing," Alonzo said "Mikael gave me that idea at my old house so I wanted one here."
"It's romantic."
"Julian and I would sit out here for hours

and plan our life."

"I am so sorry I didn't mean to..."

"That's okay it doesn't take a lot for me to cry about him."

"Alisha you will get stronger."

"I know, so how are you and Ginger."

He sat down next to me. "I leave in a few weeks so I will be gone for a few months come home for two weeks and go back in a few weeks."

"I asked about Ginger not your work schedule." I laughed

"I don't want to be with her sometimes but I feel guilty so I stay."

"You're guilty of doing what?"

"I hurt her when I dumped her in high school and she hasn't been the same since."

"Alonzo that was over twenty years ago."

"I know but she waited and saved herself for me, Alisha"

"And you believe that." I knew he was making that comment to hurt me because I married Julian.

"Why would she lie and go through so much trouble to get and keep me."

"Don't make the same mistake with her that you made with me follow your heart as God leads you not your mom or flesh."

Alonzo stood up. "I guess I'll go down stairs and sleep in my dad's room."

"Alonzo you can sleep in one of the guest rooms."

"It might not look right."

"You know I could care less about that." I walked in as he opened the door.

"Good night Alonzo."

"Good night Alisha."

Tommy's in-laws were staying for two weeks but Isabella went into labor so her brothers and friend went back. Her parents stay ended up being a week longer for her dad and two weeks for her mom. I was only around to take them out to dinner and when Isabella had the babies to shuttle them back and forth to the hospital. They had girls one was named Carrie Marie and the other one was Elise Isabel. They had named them after our grandparents. I was excited but sadden as well because Julian wanted to have one more child before it was too late and I lost our too late. Tommy worked from home most days but when his in-laws were there he went in everyday and a half day on Friday

After a while I threw myself into my work. Six months later no one asked about the baby and I didn't tell anyone I had lost it because it was obvious. I spent most of my time at the old house and Tommy hated it. Alonzo came over one evening to talk to me about slowing down and his wedding after he got back in the country. Alonzo had decided to marry Ginger after the baby was born because he would be in town for at least two weeks. We knew the real reason was that he wanted a blood test but she grew on him and he wanted to marry her and hoped that the baby was his. Alonzo and I talked for hours but it seemed like minutes. Alonzo looked at me and leaned over as I melted in his arms before I knew it he was pulling off my clothes. Alonzo and I ended up in my room like old times. After we were done he jumped up and left. I got up ashamed of my actions and dressed to go home. As I was driving home my phone rung, "Hey Tommy and yes I'm on my way home."

He laughed "I was just checking on you to make sure."

"I'm okay and thanks for checking on me Tommy."

"You're welcome Alisha." I could hear him smiling. "You know I love you."

"I love you too Tommy." We hung up and it rung again. "Tommy I told you I'm on the way home."

"This isn't Tommy."

"Alonzo?"

"Yes." He sighed "I just wanted to apologize

for running out on you like that."

"Alonzo I understand you're with Ginger."

"That's not it ." he paused as he remembered Julian's words that day he got drunk after finding Ginger was pregnant. "I didn't want to take advantage of you while you're vulnerable."

"Alonzo I knew what I was doing."

"Alisha I still love you but I can't take you leaving me again so I am going to be with Ginger." He knew Julian wanted me to be with a confident and secure man who would never hurt me.

"Alonzo I…"

"Alisha no I can't do this with you again."

"Do what?"

"Allow you to be my everything. When you married Julian I was devastated but I had Ginger running after me. When I saw that you were pregnant it broke me and I couldn't be with another woman and I still can't."

"But you just had sex with me and Ginger is pregnant."

"Alisha I've never penetrated Ginger or let her give me head without using a condom."

"But she's pregnant."

"I was drunk and I can't remember what I did that night I just know what she told me."

"But…"

"I know Alisha, shit I've never kissed Ginger."

"Are you saying I was the last woman you were with?"

"Yes."

"Alisha, I will always be in love with you but I know I can't be with you."

"Alonzo I wish you and her the best."

A few months later the kids came over to have lunch with me and Ms. Daniels and Mr. Avery. When they left Ms. Daniels forgot to lock the door behind her after putting the kids in the car to take them home. I was in my office finishing up some paperwork but couldn't concentrate because I kept seeing Julian's face. Through tears I prayed but couldn't shake the fact I was alone even though I tried to live right and allow God to guide me. My thoughts were interrupted because I heard something so I got up and walked out of my office. I bumped in to Malcolm "What are you doing here?" I asked in shock.

"Baby I want you back" he said dropping to one knee with a single pink rose.

"Malcolm I'm with Ju....." I remembered Julian was gone so I broke down in tears. "Alisha I'm not just going to walk away this time" he picked me up and threw me on the sofa. Malcolm snatched my legs open and buried his head. I was in denial until I felt his tongue and remembered why I fell in love with him. "Stop Malcolm" I said pushing him away in my mind but it felt so good that as I tried to push him away I rolled my hips to meet his tongue until I gave him my essence arching my back in pleasure.

"Baby I have a condom please let me feel you again" he said pulling his pants down and pulling the condom over his throbbing manhood.

"No" I half-heartedly exclaimed but Malcolm knew me so he snatched me to the floor and thrust himself into me as hard as he could. I tried to get up but he put his weight on me and continued. "Please stop Malcolm you're hurting me." I whimpered as I tried to push him off me.

"Baby I'm cum...."He couldn't speak just grunt in pleasure. When he finished Malcolm got up and kissed me "Give me another chance Alisha." He asked resting beside me.

"Malcolm leave" I said sternly without looking at him.

Malcolm firmly stated, "No I'm not giving up my family again." He held my hand and kissed it as he said, "Let me back into your life. You've had time to mourn now it's time to move forward."

I was so lonely and I remembered the good times with him but most of all that which drove me, the sex; he was the only man that satisfied me sexually. I kissed Malcolm and said, "I will continue to have sex with you but I don't want a relationship. I pushed his head towards my desire as he slowly caressed my passion I held his head and I spread my legs wider and released my essence harder than ever before. "Damn I forgot how hard you cum." He muttered between each lick and kiss on my thighs. "Malcolm you need to leave for real." I said quickly jumping up.

"I want to spend the night with you." He pleaded.

"The kids are spending the weekend with their grandparents so you can take me somewhere." I said as I looked into his eyes.

"May I see Milagro first?" He smiled.

"Give me time Malcolm." I said feeling ashamed of my actions as reality set in. He kissed me put on his pants and left.

I drove home and thought what I am doing. The thought of me being alone clouded my judgment. I thought about Tommy and Isabella being happily married and expecting their fourth child and last child per Isabella but Tommy wants seven. Alonzo was engaged to a due any day now

Ginger, and Mikael was living life with his spiritual wife. It's time for me to do what pleases me.

Malcolm called me while I was driving home and started talking before I could say hello. "Alisha my ex-wife came to see you because I won't have anything to do with her and she knows I'm still in love with you."
"Malcolm I want to take this thing slow because you betrayed me the last time I was with you." I said slowly waiting for his backlash.
"Baby I understand I will do whatever it takes to get you and my daughter back." He said patiently. I was in shock because the Malcolm I knew was an unreasonable man that became hateful if you didn't comply with his wishes.
"Malcolm you seem different." I said with a hint of surprise in my tone.
He calmly said, "Alisha I've had a lot of time to think and I know what you mean to me." He sighed "I know what my children mean to me now because I was not there and missed so much that they won't have anything to do with me." He sounded as if he wanted to cry. "I have a chance to make things right with my soul mate and my beautiful daughter."

I smiled and thought maybe he has changed but something within my soul was unsettled and caused my stomach to quiver. "Malcolm this is the start of something new."

We hung up and a thought ran through my mind. "Did you seek God first?" I shook it off but another thought flew into my mind. "Is this your fleshly desire or God's perfect will?" I pulled over and cried out, "Lord, can I please have this moment because I'm so lonely and I don't want to be alone right now!"
I felt a comfort in my spirit that said, "You're not alone because I am always with you but you choose to dwell in what the world tells you." I cried because the revelation came from God but I was caught up in my flesh and made the decision to be with Malcolm.

That morning when I checked my answering machine Julian's father Mike called me. His message was confusing because he said Rasheda was dating the devil and Derek was in a relationship with the evil one and he believed they had something to do with Julian's death but the guys are not talking without a deal. I called him back but he never answered.

I made a decision to follow my flesh seeking an unrealistic and known hurtful fulfillment. Will I ever wake up and see the revelation God freely gives?

When we beg or choose something God says is bad for us the painful lesson is our own fault. The unnecessary journey we chose to take against the will of God is foolish and the pain and hurt from those things could've been avoided but the flesh wants what the flesh wants. God can use that hurt to strengthen and teach you but it is best to follow God in the first place.

www.ingramcontent.com/pod-product-compliance
Lightning Source LLC
Chambersburg PA
CBHW070853250626
47159CB00003B/1043